I0552260

# The Adultery Code

## Lizzie Bow

Grosvenor House
Publishing Limited

This book is published by
Grosvenor House Publishing Ltd
Link House
140 The Broadway, Tolworth, Surrey, KT6 7HT.
www.grosvenorhousepublishing.co.uk

This book is a work of fiction. Any resemblance to
people or events, past or present, is purely coincidental.

A CIP record for this book
is available from the British Library

Paperback ISBN  978-1-83615-429-7

# 'To *the* reader'

As you begin to read the next few pages and paragraphs, it is possible that you may very quickly form an opinion of Sarah.

My hope is that, if you still hold that opinion as you make your way through the book and Sarah's journey through her decisions, you will have gained some empathy with her predicament and maybe see, understand and appreciate her reasons. But that doesn't mean you have to agree or disagree.

Whatever your past or present personal circumstances, from whichever side of the story you are reading this, there are descriptions of events that you may have experienced or wished you had.

Thank you
Lizzie x

As I put on the final touch of lipstick my, I felt every possible emotion – excitement, apprehension, urging, longing and guilt – I felt every emotion except the one I should have felt... regret.

I was fully aware of the consequences and risks that the next couple of hours held and I knew all too well that at any second during that time I could prevent any such consequence and eradicate any such risks. But I was being driven by an inexplicable force.

As I got into my car I opened my phone to be greeted by a picture of myself and my husband on our wedding day some 15 years earlier, second time around for both of us. On the home screen was a picture of my family on one of our family weekends – both pictures of happiness and contentment.

I was checking that I was going to be on time and that there were no messages of cancellation for my afternoon arrangement. I quickly closed the cover on my phone as if to shut out the reality of my present life.

A tiny part of me would have breathed a sigh of relief if there had been a message of cancellation but I could equally have cancelled this arrangement, but I just couldn't be the decider on this.

So, I drove away from my house as I had done thousands of times before, but this time was different, very different. This time I wasn't leaving to go to work or the supermarket. This time I was on my way to meet another man.

Someone who had occupied my thoughts for many years but only from afar.

I first saw him, or should I say heard him, when he was one of the managers in the office where I worked. His voice was deep and commanding and our initial introduction was uneventful. Yet for some reason, to me, there was something about him and for some equally unknown reason every time I heard his voice the butterflies in my stomach would attack again and again and I felt this desperate need to be somehow closer to him, anywhere in his vicinity. It was as if his presence fed an insatiable need in me.

He worked across the county and the times that we were together in the same place were limited to once or twice a month. He came to a colleague's retirement do at our office on one occasion and in that more informal atmosphere he was a little more relaxed with everyone and for the first time I was able to exchange more than a couple of words in conversation with him. However, I detected no signal that he was feeling the same butterflies that consumed me, quite the contrary. He was accompanied by his wife and at that moment, seeing her towering elegance and their obvious connection together, I realised that any butterflies on my part were completely misplaced.

At least I hadn't embarrassed myself so, head held high, off I went home.

On the face of it, if I described my life at home to a stranger it would seem almost ideal. Indeed, to anyone who had a bad marriage or money worries it would seem perfect. I had none of these and together with a lovely home that was all paid for, working because I wanted to and not for financial reasons. I had my own money so didn't have any restriction's when it came to buying clothes, etc. My children – two from my first marriage – were all grown up and settled into their own lives.

My husband was nearly ten years older than me and had seemingly, without a word of objection, provided me with a very good life. He is a lovely gentle man who had me and my family at the centre of his world.

Of course, we had our arguments over the years and the normal ups and downs, but these were mostly resolved quickly.

Now in our later years we have become very comfortable in each other's company. The proverbial old pair of slippers.

Intimacy had long since left our relationship save for the very occasional fumbling attempt which was rarely completed and usually was eventually given up as a bad job. It was a need that as a couple we no longer felt added anything to our relationship.

I did masturbate sometimes but I never knew whether my husband still did, I rarely thought of sex as an act anymore.

We had an understanding of each other which comes with the years spent together.

My life was good, very good, but incomplete emotionally, unfulfilled mentally and unstimulated sexually.

A few years went by and life went on in its regimented and predictable way. Good times, bad times, sad times and times of joy had all made an appearance and were embraced and overcame as the situation demanded.

I heard that he had left the company after a couple of years and I myself had gained a promotion and moved offices.

The day didn't feel any different to any other day that I had prepared to get ready for work. The dog ran off when I had walked him earlier and having to find him in the park had made me slightly later than planned into work but nothing out of the ordinary.

Would I have done anything differently if I had known or even had an inkling of the events that were about to unfold and would serve to make this the last 'ordinary' day that I would have?

Parking in my usual spot in the car park, I made my way into the building and up to the first floor using the lift. It was Monday and as usual I was laden down with a couple of heavy bags and a lunch box. I headed for the central room where it was normal Monday morning practice to hold a team briefing to plan out the work for the week ahead.

There was a little hustling noise that I had noticed from other team members and my colleague said that she had heard that we were getting a new manager and he or she was going to be introduced to us this morning. Our usual manager had been ill for some time and I had also heard talk of there being a temporary replacement until his health had improved.

I recognised the 'clip clop' of the secretary's heels on the wooden floor as she made her way to the central room and I instantly knew the voice that was accompanying her even before the face appeared. The butterflies, the churning knots in my stomach, and for some reason the feeling of panic – almost fight or flight mode had set in – returned as if a switch had been turned on.

During the next few seconds I shuffled in my chair, crossed and uncrossed my legs I don't know how many times, but I felt completely incoherent.

Then there he was – standing in the same room as me, in my vicinity once again. I didn't hear the introduction to the group; I was frozen mentally and physically.

Colleagues left their seats to welcome our new arrival and have the obligatory handshake; I was unable to move a limb. I felt my heart would jump out of my throat and was really struggling to compose myself, let alone a sentence.

The room quietened as colleagues made their welcomes and then left to return to their respective desks and offices. Then the voice. "Hello," he said, "I think we have worked together before unless I am mistaken."

With a broken, quivering voice I replied, "Yes I think so, my name is Sarah Peel." I put my now very sweaty palm forward to shake his hand and our hands touched. The connection was made. I have carried that feeling with me ever since that morning.

He had never before given me such attention and I desperately tried not to read much, if anything, into the enthusiasm (or so it seemed to me), although mild, with which he had greeted me. It was, to my mind, on a much elevated level from anything that we had exchanged in our earlier connections.

Concentration was difficult throughout the rest of the day although I didn't see him that much as the usual round of meetings and introductions that come with starting a new job took up most of his day.

My day was spent with 50 percent work stuff and the other 50 percent trying to convince myself that he must be aware of the connection between us. This feeling, for me, was so strong, so obvious, that it couldn't be just mine; maybe he too was having the same internal battle, maybe he was just as confused by it and maybe he was just waiting for a signal from me. Maybe, maybe, maybe...! Then again, maybe not, maybe it was and always had been in my head, my little escapism from my slightly boring yet really, quite fine everyday existence.

How would I know, how would he know, how would anyone know, what if anyone did know? How, how, how...?

Home time arrived and usually my drive home would be occupied with thoughts of whether the dog walker had remembered to give the dog his usual treat, or if I should have hung the washing out after all this morning, should I stop at the supermarket to get something for tea, or did I have enough in the fridge to put together something edible. Blah, blah, blah... My head was now swimming with thoughts of what I should wear tomorrow, which perfume and, among all of these things, how much makeup to wear and would I be too obvious if I made these changes in my appearance?

One thing that I was certain of was that whatever I chose to wear, or however I chose to look, my husband certainly wouldn't notice let alone comment on it.

Most evenings after work and dog walking, which I usually did alone, I would change into my pyjamas. Gone were the days of wearing anything alluring for bed, in fact these were quite shapeless efforts and had been renamed as my 'floppies'. After the usual round of clearing away after tea and some mini tidying up, by 9pm I would be on the sofa, more often than not with a glass of something and flicking through the television channels to find something to entertain us for the next hour or so. My husband would have adopted this position a while before I did, especially if there was any football or sport on the television. Howsoever it happened, there we would sit, opposite ends of the sofa with barely a word of conversation exchanged between us.

However, as with the day, this was not an ordinary evening.

Instead of heading for the sofa, I scuttled my way upstairs to the spare room where I kept my special, not every day, outfits. I busily fumbled through blouse after blouse, skirt after skirt and dress after dress. What colour, which style, fitted or not? Almost a sense of panic had befallen me. Then, momentarily, I would stop and take a breath and the reality of what I was doing and why I was doing it and what I was planning would weigh me down. In that moment, I would try to convince myself of how stupid I was being and how futile my efforts would turn out to be as there had not been, up to now, absolutely any indication at all that all of this wouldn't be in vain.

I was in effect preening myself and aiming to put myself on display to attract someone that quite possibly hadn't let me enter his head since our encounter at the team briefing earlier that day.

Eventually I picked out a skirt and blouse and paraded myself in front of the mirror adopting every possible pose when I noticed that my blouse gaped at the bust, must have gained a few pounds since I last wore it. So, starting again, I spotted a dress and jacket, blue and black respectively. I also chose some shoes that I hadn't worn since my daughter's wedding, although I knew that by wearing them my feet would be killing me by mid-morning. I felt they completed my outfit so they were going on my feet regardless.

Bedtime came and went but it was far from a restful night for me.

My husband was walking our dog on this morning so that gave me some extra time to spend on my appearance.

I would describe my hair as quite boring and plain really, a layered bob with a few highlights to cover the ensuing grey and I wouldn't normally take that much time over it for a day at work. This morning though I it smothered in a cloud of dry shampoo in an effort to introduce some tousled volume and reduce the plain and straight style.

Everything about me was different today, then it crossed my mind that maybe he wouldn't even be in the office or even in the building today – my stomach sank at the thought, and I had the feeling that a child would get if their best friend hadn't come to school.

Funnily enough, when I arrived at my work, my usual parking spot had already been taken as if to emphasise the beginning of a new chapter. I was overthinking everything again.

I hadn't noticed anyone else around me as I approached the door to the office building when, from nowhere, someone said, "Let me get that for you." I didn't need to look up to see who the voice belonged to as I was in no doubt as to its identity. An arm reached from behind me and we both giggled at one another when he realised that the doors were in fact automatic and had opened before he could put his hand on it. In this momentary exchange, our eyes met properly for the first time. It was a longer than expected look, but I couldn't say why.

Once inside, I headed towards the lift; I didn't want to walk for any longer than I needed to in these shoes. At this point he said that he would take the stairs and we parted. I cannot remember the short journey in the lift, I think there were other people in it with me. I came out of my daze as the lift pinged at my floor. I made my way to my desk and quickly sat down seeking a few moments to gather my thoughts.

Had he noticed my hair, my makeup, my dress or my shoes – all so different from the day before. Who knows, how could I know, how would I be able to tell if any of my extra efforts had been noticed?

I reached for my phone from my handbag and checked for any messages and was greeted with the usual picture of myself and my husband on our wedding day – it was like a reminder, a memory-jerker that I was a married woman.

On this day I had arranged to leave work at 3pm as I had an appointment for a massage – a gift from my children last Christmas which I had only just got around to using. Up until 3pm, the day passed uneventfully.

The evening was also pretty much routine except for the utter mush that my thought processes had turned into.

The following day I kept an eye out for him as I parked my car and made my way into the building but no sign of him so far. Again, I had chosen an outfit that I felt a little more attractive in, but I had begun to wonder how long I could keep up this level of effort with my appearance, at least without the reward of any reciprocated attention.

I logged into my computer to check for any emails that may have landed in my inbox since me leaving work early yesterday.

I was totally distracted from the last couple of messages as I was drawn to an email that had come through at 4:30pm yesterday as it had his name as the sender – Anthony Randall.

I stared at my computer screen for what seemed like ages as I deliberated as to what the message could be. Was this the sign that I had been longing for? The anticipation was crushing but then so was the possibility of disappointment – the longer I left it unread the longer I had hope.

Tentatively opening the message, the first few words made it clear that the possibility of disappointment had proved to be true. It was an email introducing himself to everyone which had been sent to everyone. Another slam in the stomach.

There wasn't much time to think about much else but work up until lunchtime, so my thoughts were preoccupied with that.

Suddenly the familiar 'ding' of an incoming email caught my attention. I raised my eyes from my desk and could barely contain my inner excitement when I saw it was from Anthony. I tempered myself and reminded myself that this could be another group email communication and that again I was only one of a crowd. But then 'Hi Sarah' were the opening words so no, not a group email, this one was for me and me alone. I read and reread it countless times.

*Hi Sarah. I expect you received my communal email yesterday afternoon along with everyone else, however, I am aware that official introductions between us are not strictly necessary, but the email had gone before I knew it (rolling eye emoji).*

I really couldn't decide whether to reply, let alone *what* to reply. It was only just after lunchtime, so I decided, in an effort not to look too eager, to take my time before replying.

There was very little else on my mind for the next couple of hours as I reread his email over and over again, trying to decipher the meaning that may or may not be contained within, and becoming aware that other pressing matters and responses to do with work were getting put further and further back.

And then the voice – he was here. I heard his voice, and he was talking to one of my colleagues – I purposely didn't look up from my screen when he unexpectedly made his way over to my desk.

"Sarah," he said. I was transfixed on the sound of him saying my name for a few seconds, so much so that I almost missed the following part of his sentence. "I thought you mustn't be in today as I hadn't heard back from you. Anyway, sorry you just got the group email. I didn't want you to think I'd forgotten that we knew each other already."

So, had he, like me, been trawling his inbox, waiting, watching and hoping for a reply from me? He had to repeat his following sentence twice. Now I was in a complete blur. "How long have you worked in this department?" I remember the question, but I cannot remember my answer. But it was most likely some ridiculous garbled response. He told me that the reason for his personal visit was to invite anyone who could make it to an informal coffee morning to be held in the main central room tomorrow. So, once again, I was being grouped along with everyone else, so everything I had read into and hoped had been the reason behind his personal office visit was once again all in my head. I think I nodded in acceptance to his group coffee meeting and then he was gone.

It was a very rare occasion when my husband and I had evening arrangements, but tonight was one of those evenings, having been invited to a neighbours' house for dinner and drinks. They lived within walking distance from our house so we could both enjoy a glass of wine or two although my husband rarely drank. The evening was lovely with lovely food and interesting conversation, discussing or rather gossiping about other people in our village and random current affairs. The men were chewing over the latest sports fixtures and results. All seemed well with my world and the different faces and environment were a distraction from what had recently become my usual evening thoughts.

I must have had more to drink than I thought, or maybe the drinks were stronger than I thought. But the following morning my head felt so heavy that I could barely lift it from the pillow, so I elected to stay in bed for another couple of hours in an effort to ease my hangover, I hadn't had one of them for a while. After a short sleep and a mug of tea and the two obligatory paracetamol was brought up to me by my husband, I managed to get up and shower and for the first time in a few weeks I didn't pay that much attention to what I would wear. I was already late for work, so I had to get a move on, our office practiced flexi working time for those who needed it or preferred it so I would have had to work late or make up the hours at some time.

I wasn't aware that anyone had noticed my unusually late arrival. When I got into my desk, there was a buzz of conversation around the office and I overheard a couple of people commenting on the informal office chat with Anthony this morning, which I had missed. To be honest, in my hangover haze, it had completely slipped my mind. I don't know whether he would have noticed that I was missing, but I decided that once I had logged into my computer, I would send a courtesy email of apology. Of course, I wouldn't confess to my hangover being the cause of my absenteeism. Instead, I would blame the dog, the car or the traffic. So off it went as follows.

*Andrew* (even that salutation put me in a quandary. Maybe I should address him as Mr Randall? Never mind, sticking with Andrew), *please accept my apologies for my nonattendance to your meeting this morning. I was in a little later than planned due to an emergency vet appointment. Sorry I missed the coffee.*

All a complete lie, a complete fabrication that I cannot explain. Now I'd have to remember, if I was ever asked again, that the dog needed treatment. Why, why, why am I creating this facade? It is as if I am becoming two different people living two parallel but different lives. But then I convinced myself that I am not doing and have not done anything wrong. On the face of it, I have felt some sort of connection with another man which may be or most likely is not mutual.

So the email was sent and I settled into my usual routine of reading and responding to various emails, making and taking telephone calls when the ding of another email caught my eye. Well, at least the sender's name caught my eye. It was from Anthony Randall. I hesitated yet again before finally opening it. It started, 'Hello again, Sarah', so it was just for me and I eagerly read on.

*Thank you for your message and I too am sorry that you couldn't make it to this morning's meeting. I am also sorry that your dog needed attention at the vet and I hope there is nothing too serious to worry about.*

I could barely catch my breath when I continued to read his next couple of lines.

*You missed a constructive meeting and some very nice coffee, maybe you and I can catch up over a coffee soon.*

The words almost jumped off the screen as I tried to read or not read any sort of meaning into it. Could this be a personal or even private invitation, or was it simply a common courtesy reply to my email? And how on earth was I to reply and respond? I didn't want to reply too quickly as I didn't want to look too eager, but I also didn't want to leave it too long to reply as the moment could be lost. Besides, I hadn't composed myself enough to put together a coherent sentence. Eventually I managed to come up with a sentence, all five words of it.

*I look forward to that.*

And click, it was gone. Had I sounded too eager, too forward? Only time would tell. I started to feel an urgent need to get out of the office as I anticipated the look on his face if I had taken his email completely out of context. Lying again, I made the excuse of having to pick the dog up from the vets to escape from the office early. I was sweating and inwardly panicking and was somehow relieved when I finally got into my car.

As I arrived home earlier than planned and managed to get my thoughts in order before the usual home evening routine was underway, and just as I had done a week or so ago, my evening thoughts were taken up with what to choose to wear tomorrow, just in case I have another face-to-face encounter.

I was still completely torn as to the meaning of it – of Anthony's email. If there was indeed any meaning, I'd flip-flop between telling myself not to be so stupid and totally convincing myself that it was a sort of 'test of the waters' type of email. Then I remembered my five-feeble-word reply and wondered if he had read it before he left work and what on earth he made of it. *Was that all she could come up with?* was probably his reaction All of this going around in my head while my lovely husband cleared away the last of the mess from the tea. You would have thought that would have brought me right back to reality, but no, I was lost once again in my own world of fantasy. But then again, was it fantasy? Here I go again.

The morning arrives and I'm sorted as I make my way to work. I had decided that today must be a day of concentration as far as work was concerned, as owing to my short day yesterday and my general distraction, I needed to catch up on outstanding matters. I anticipated at least one further email from Anthony today, although I had no idea why and even deludingly decided that I would ignore them until I was ahead with my other commitments. Now I was thinking like I was in control. *As if!*

Anyway, that plan was all in vain as I received no such communication on that day or on the next, in fact no sight or sound of him for the rest of the week. And then the weekend arrived with a break from the outfit-planning and early morning hair titivation. I found myself somewhat liberated. The weekend was spent pleasantly doing nice things with family and friends.

Anthony frequently jumped into my head as I pictured his weekend spent doing more interesting things than I had done and I wondered – assumed that he would have at some point over the weekend – if he'd had sex with his wife. I pictured the whole scenario in my head. How it would play out. The ambient lighting, the music, food and the wine. I pictured it all. The gentle teasing conversation, the lingering eye contact filled with promise. And then the touch, skin to skin contact and the mingling of each other's breath. In that very few minutes, I felt a real urge to masturbate, get it out of my system but there wasn't the opportunity, at least not during the day.

All of the things that had been a part of my life at some time were played out again in my mind, as I knew only too well that in my present, pleasant existence there was zero possibility of any of them ever reoccurring. I had forgone lust and passion for comfort and ease but isn't that what everyone does eventually?

During the occasions when I felt the need to fulfil myself sexually, it never crossed my mind to approach my husband and maybe give him the signal of my desires. It wasn't that he wasn't fanciable, quite the opposite as he still drew attention from women when we were in other company. He was a nice, gentle, sociable, friendly man, a really good companion and I don't doubt that he always had my best interests at heart, it's just that he didn't really show any sexual interest anymore. Kisses were always pecks on the cheek. We had even stopped giving each other a kiss or a peck at bedtime. Whatever was there sexually between us had faded long ago, and whether we noticed it or not, neither of us consciously decided to discuss it or do anything about it. It had been replaced by an imaginary comfort blanket that kept myself, my home and family safe and warm. I wouldn't know, and I certainly had no indication, that he still masturbated and whether he did was it me or us that instigated it, or was it porn? I just didn't know and felt no desire to enquire.

Part of me was worried about the can of worms that might open up if I attempted the conversation. Maybe I would find out that he didn't fancy me, or maybe, like me, he had desires for another woman as I had for another man. After digesting that thought, I would be lying if I didn't admit to feeling a little envy that another woman would have the company of this lovely man.

But did I actually have the right to have any opinion on the matter given how I have conducted myself over the past couple of weeks to gain the attention of someone else? I hated myself in at that moment and the reality of what I was contemplating really was beginning to hit home. The remaining question was, was I going to do anything about it?

On Monday morning I wasn't at work as I had booked the day off to treat myself to a manicure and pedicure and get my eyebrows done. Much to my beautician's surprise, I opted for a completely different nail colour, not my usual safe coral. This time I chose the brightest, shiniest red. "What's with the change?" she asked curiously. "Special occasion?"

Taken aback by her questions I spat out, "Not really, just fancied a change," and in that moment it crossed my mind that maybe she knew, maybe she could tell. After all, she dealt with people all day who may have ulterior motives for a change in their usual routine. Then I thought, but that is exactly what this is. I do indeed have an ulterior motive, and it was at moments like these when a tinge of guilt set in – the feeling that everyone around me from the delivery driver, the doctors' receptionist and the beautician somehow knew. I couldn't hide it, it was written all over my face.

Guilt turned to panic so, in an effort to redeem myself, the rest of our conversation consisted of dribbling talk about my home and family life. *That should put paid to any suspicions*, I thought. All of this over the fact that I had changed my nail colour – now I really was going mad.

Over the next couple of days at work, I flashed my new nails and also hid them in equal measure as if I was playing two different roles.

Role one: I was using every possible female charm that I possessed to gain the attention of someone who may have absolutely no interest in me whatsoever.

Role two: the guilty pleasures lady. Only I knew the reason for these beautiful nails but was convinced that by showing them off I was giving away my secret so, when possible, I kept them hidden.

What was going on in my head? However, no sign of Anthony on either Tuesday or Wednesday so the nails had been a waste of time on these days.

I felt somehow calmer on Thursday and had been at my desk for a couple of hours when another one of those group emails popped into my inbox. It was from

Anthony to everyone informing us all that next week he was taking prearranged annual leave and therefore wouldn't be back into the office until Monday week. I read it and read it and read it again, deciding whether to reply. On the face of it, it didn't call for a reply. It was a statement, not a question. As I realised that this would be my final communication with him until his return, I gingerly responded and, acknowledging his email, I wished him a good holiday. His response came within the hour.

*Thanks Sarah, I haven't forgotten. I owe you a coffee. We need to arrange that.*

I replied.

*Oh yes catch me on your return.*

That didn't seem over the top. The best I could hope for was a public coffee next to the coffee machine and that is what I had in mind would happen. However, his reply, which was swift, was completely out of the blue.

*I don't have to be at work to buy you a coffee. Maybe we could arrange something during my week off?*

I looked at it time and time again. Then suddenly another message.

*My mobile number might make things easier.*

And there it was – his number. I had a direct contact number with him now. No more waiting for emails. I didn't answer. I couldn't answer. My legs had turned to jelly, my eyes were in disbelief at what I had just read and I felt at that moment everyone around me knew what I had and what had just happened. The panic, the shame, the guilt and the absolute pleasure of it all consumed me completely.

I hurriedly put his number into my phone contacts but for some reason I put him under the name of 'Andrea R' – why had I chosen to do that? I have several phone numbers from men in my contacts list – friends, colleagues, hairdresser – all men and all listed under their own name. Was I afraid, or anticipating, an inappropriate message, inappropriate for a married woman to receive?

In any case my husband has never and would never dream of looking at any of my messages, I was completely confident of that and I had no reason or desire to ever look at his phone. Our mobile phones were just left lying around at home. We never had the feeling or suspicion that one of us might have something to hide, something that we wouldn't want the other to see so this act of deception that I had just displayed was bewildering at the least.

It dawned on me that this was his last working day before his break and I couldn't decide whether to reply before he left work or wait until his return, certainly the 'let's have coffee' invitation contained a suggestion of a meeting during his time off.

So, putting myself at the risk of embarrassment and rejection, I took the bull by the horns and sent him a WhatsApp message. What on earth did we do before we had this facility? This was also an underhand way of letting him have my number without being too obvious and actually offering it. I messaged, 'Hello Anthony (waving hand emoji) thanks for your number. I have added you to my WhatsApp contacts list if that's ok with you' and I signed off as Sarah Peel.

I sent it and wondered if he had the 'read receipt' option on his WhatsApp setting on his phone so I know by the 'blue tick' whether and when he had read my message. Well, I didn't have to wait for very long as the 'blue ticks' appeared almost immediately. A sudden gush of embarrassment overtook me and I kept reading the message that I had sent, searching for any possible hidden intentions in its construction. It seemed pretty innocent to me and although I had written it to exude a hidden meaning, I was still searching for that signal from him without giving away a signal from me – could I make this any more complicated?

So, a minute went by, then two, then five. I knew he had received and read my message so why was it taking him so long to reply? Minutes seemed vital somehow. Maybe I had done the wrong thing and appearing to be so familiar was a step too far. But why would that be as he had offered his number to me in the first place, so what was I supposed to do with it? Questions coupled with anxieties were building up.

Then came his reply.

As with his first email to me a few weeks ago, I didn't open it immediately. I actually considered disabling the 'read receipt' function on my phone at this point to give me the opportunity to read it without him knowing, digest it and construct a suitable response without the pressure of time. I was also trying not to give the impression that I was glued to my phone and that I actually did have an interesting and full life with lots of friends and interests which meant that my phone and messages on it were secondary considerations. Another complete lie. My phone had now become a direct connection to him 24/7 so no more weekend and out of office hours breaks in contact.

I decided that a wait of five minutes was an acceptable length of time before opening his reply and I wondered if he had felt as anxious as I did whilst waiting for the 'blue ticks'.

'Absolutely that's a great idea' was his reply and that was it. Not sure what to make of it, I decided not to reply.

All of that distraction had taken another half an hour out of my work time so once again I was becoming delayed with work stuff so I needed to concentrate on that for the rest of the day.

It had crossed my mind that Anthony and I would not communicate via mobile phone again unless it was work-related, so I put my phone on silent and popped it into my handbag to eliminate the distraction – who was I kidding?

I must have looked at my phone a dozen times in an hour just looking for any other messages and constantly going over his messages. There were a couple of other messages, one from my daughter moaning about her boss at work and one from my husband to let me know that he was going to do some gardening for a neighbour, and he was unlikely to be home when I got in from work. He was also taking the dog with him so as not for me to worry about his whereabouts. Such a lovely consideration but I didn't reply to either of them just then.

The weekend came and went without much change to the usual routine. I eventually got around to a phone call chat with my daughter and I listened maternally as she filled me in with problems at her place of work, nothing serious really, just her boss changing things around and risking a mutiny in the office.

Monday morning also came around with its usual regularity, and I must admit to feeling a little relieved that I didn't have to go through my wardrobe and cupboards to find an outfit, and I left the hair straighteners well alone for the first working morning in a few weeks.

I wasn't in my usual rush to log into my computer as I wasn't anticipating any emails from Anthony that weren't work related and as the day went on that is exactly what happened – no communication from him of any sort by any means.

My drive home was also uneventful. I was feeling a little deflated. Not only had I not had any communication from Anthony, although I didn't expect to hear from him over the weekend as that was family time for both of us, but I thought that if I had been on his mind as much as he had been on mine, then at the first opportunity i.e., Monday morning, he would have made me his first contact of the day. Deflation had now turned into frustration and then to disappointment.

There was only one way of dealing with these feelings and that was my usual way of dealing with most things that I couldn't control and out came the wine glass swiftly followed by the rest of the wine left over from the weekend. This was always greeted with a look of disdain from my husband, followed by 'an over the spectacles' look at the clock as if to remind me of the time. It is typical, I think, of the reaction from anyone who leads a relatively stressless life to a make someone who prefers, or needs, a glass of something to aid relaxation after the stresses of the working day, howsoever they are caused. He would say it was a gentle reminder that I had started the evening drinking early and that he was only thinking of me. I would say it was passive bullying as, more often than not, thanks to his perceived but totally incorrect opinion of my 'excessive' alcohol consumption, I wouldn't have any more to drink during the evening. Well, not where he could see and judge me at least.

"That's early," came the response from my husband as he walked down the stairs. "Had a bad day?" he continued. He had been putting away the washing that had dried during the day.

"Not bad, just frustrating," I returned.

There was food left over from the weekend, so tea was quickly put together. I set about my evening routine. Both my husband and I took the dog for a walk, which was a rare occurrence, although aside from the occasional random comment, there was very little meaningful conversation between us.

Tuesday came... oh boy, did Tuesday come.

I had barely sat down at my desk when the familiar tone of a WhatsApp message arrived on my phone. It is exactly the same tone that sounds no matter who messages me. Yet, somehow, I knew, I could feel it, this was a message from Anthony. I quickly, furiously opened my phone and then my WhatsApp chat, and there it was, there he was – 'Andrea R'. There was no profile picture, whereas I had posted a really boring picture of a pot of flowers from my garden – pretty but not scintillating.

It read, 'Hi, how are you? I hope your working week is so far going ok'. Then, with eyes on stalks,

I read on to the next sentence. 'How about that coffee, do you have any free time this week?'. It was signed Anthony.

I gasped silently and leaned back in my chair and was in a momentary state of disbelief when the butterflies returned, fluttering so hard that I swear everyone could see them but as I looked around the office it seemed everyone was just getting on with their work and no one was paying any attention to me at all.

Then the situation with the blue ticks overcame me. Would he know that I had opened and read his message within two minutes of sending it? I didn't want to seem too keen, too desperate, but I didn't want to appear standoffish either and I didn't want to lose the moment, as it were.

I actually don't know how I managed to do it, but I held off for about half an hour before replying. Half an hour seemed a respectable time distance, but I don't know where I got that idea from and it felt like hours.

So, I replied, 'Hello Anthony lovely to hear from you. Coffee sounds good, can I get back to you later today when I have had a chance to look at my diary?'. Then I signed off 'Sarah'.

'Sort my diary'… who was I kidding? Trying to make it sound as if I had other interesting things to do and as if I wouldn't drop everything and anything to share this coffee. As if, as if.

The blue ticks indicated that he had read my message, and he replied, 'Of course, let me know when you are sorted and get back to me, I look forward to it.' This time he signed off as 'Ax'.

I focused entirely on that last bit: 'Ax'. What on earth was I supposed to make of it? I even scribbled it a few times on my notepad.

I had a couple of interviews to conduct as the company was recruiting two apprentices to join the team and so, for the most part, I was distracted by those.

Anthony, and his messages, were on my mind for most of the rest of the morning and I wondered whether I had crossed his mind from time to time.

The interviews had taken up most of the rest of the morning and after the obligatory post-interview meetings with more senior staff, who would make the final decision on appointments, it was nearly lunchtime by the time I got back to my desk. The first thing I did was reach for my phone but, to my disappointment, there were no further messages from Anthony, in fact there were no messages from anyone. I don't know why I thought Anthony would have messaged me as he was waiting for a response from me – the ball was in my court so to speak. So I played with my pen for a few minutes trying to look busy, but I decided to send him a reply. 'Hi again. I should have some free time this Friday afternoon if that suits you'. And again, I signed off as Sarah.

I really now needed to skip lunch and get on with dealing with the other emails that had clustered in my inbox during the morning. So, a coffee and a bag of Maltesers on my desk was my lunch. Although I had put my phone away in my handbag in an effort to detach myself from it, I was constantly on alert for the vibration and/or tone of a received message.

I did get myself immersed into some important emails and telephone calls and I was surprised at how the time flew by given I would be leaving for home within the next hour.

I had had no response to my Friday afternoon offering for coffee. I could see that he had read my message, and the lack of a reply had made me feel a little deflated. Just before I left work for home another message came through. 'Hi Sarah, I hope I have caught you before you leave work. Friday pm is good for me too (thumbs up emoji), shall we discuss tomorrow time and place (another thumbs up emoji)? Have a good evening'. And signed again 'Ax'.

I read the message a couple of times again and then it came to me that, as he had mentioned he wanted to catch me before I left for work, he was consciously not wanting or expecting us to communicate with each other outside of office hours so our arrangements would not encroach into our personal and private lives. It was as if we were holding some sort of secret, but was I overthinking again?

As the prospect of all of this swam around my head, I thought of it in another way. He contacted me only during office hours as I didn't mean anything to him outside of work and I didn't form any part of his thoughts when he wasn't working. I settled myself with the latter explanation and consoled my inner thoughts with the fact that, in my head, I wasn't actually doing anything wrong.

Funny how every cell in your body is screaming out to you to stop and think before things go far. Your head and your heart conflict against each other until, finally, they both tell you, make you think and make you believe that all will be well.

My husband had gone to meet up with a few of his gardening club pals and my evening was consumed with my outfit, hair and makeup for the Friday afternoon coffee meet-up with Anthony, even though the final arrangements hadn't yet been made.

As I sat at my desk the next morning, I couldn't really tell from his last message whether he would be expecting the first contact from me today or whether it meant that he was going to initiate the communications, so I decided to wait until lunchtime to see if anything had happened.

I really couldn't think of anywhere to go. There wasn't a list of meeting places for married women to meet married men to refer to – maybe a gap in the market there – although I am sure someone has already thought of it, it's just that I had never had the need to seek it out before. I thought to myself and gave a wry smile, *or maybe there is a reason such a list doesn't exist... because it shouldn't be needed!* For some reason, however, when I did get an idea, I was considering places that were not near to home or work. By doing this I was already adding a level of secrecy but my reasons for this were not rational. On the face of it I had accepted an invitation to meet up for coffee with a colleague, it must happen millions of times a day all over the world, so why was I feeling that this time needed to be kept a secret?

Before I had the chance to put much more thought into anything, my phone vibrated with a message. That was another thing, why was I now keeping my phone on silent when I was at home and work? The message was predictably and thankfully, from Anthony. It read, 'Hi Sarah (waving hand emoji), any thoughts or ideas for our coffee place/time? Ax'. There was that 'Ax' again, maybe he signed off all his messages in this way and maybe it wasn't just reserved for me. In a further way not to look too eager, I waited an hour before I replied which gave me time to have a think of somewhere as he was obviously waiting for me to make the suggestions.

I did manage, as well, to send a couple of proposals that were nearly overdue to the accounts department, so I satisfied myself that I was doing some work as well. Mostly, though, that hour was spent trying to come up with a venue. A pub? A coffee shop? A park? It was difficult to select appropriately as I was still unsure of the meaning of the meeting.

A pub made it sound like a date, a walk in the park would depend on the weather, and a coffee shop made it sound like a meet-up with an old friend and I wasn't sure from his perspective which category this fell into. Then I reminded myself that whether I went or not was completely in my hands, and his, but, before I knew it, I was compiling my reply.

'Hi again – just thinking about Friday. Do you have a time in mind? I can be free from 1:30pm'.

I really wanted to sign off as 'Sx' and see what his response would have been but the coward in me reared its head, and I signed off "Sarah".

Another swift reply. 'Shall we say 2:30 then?' Then he added, 'Lady's choice so I will leave the details to you, anywhere that you feel comfortable. Ax'.

It was all starting to feel very real. I was now making plans to meet another man whom I had disguised on my phone under another name – a female name. The layers of deceit were slowly building up.

The distraction of this other life provided me something that I had lacked in my every day almost perfect existence. That is how I was feeling, as if I was living two separate lives, each one giving me what I lacked from the other. I had become two different people. In this way I was convincing myself that the person who was making these arrangements and whose thoughts were consumed by the uncertainty and excitement of the next few days wasn't really me, it was the other person, so I, in fact, was innocent.

I remembered a place where I had met a long-standing girlfriend for coffee a couple of years ago. She lived a hundred miles or so away but, until her mother passed away, she would commute monthly to make family visits, so I decided to suggest this place. 'Do you know the Terracotta Pot Garden Centre? I replied. And then I thought, *a garden centre!* It sounded so old fashioned, and I was embarrassed that I couldn't think of anywhere livelier. I was 56 years old, but I am sure I have just made myself sound 20 years older. But it was too late; the message had gone.

The rest of Tuesday went by without any further messages.

He had indicated previously, but not verbally confirmed, that our messages would only be in work hours so, disappointingly, I was pretty sure that I wouldn't hear from him again for the rest of the evening. Even so, I checked my phone again as I got into my car, and again after I had pulled up onto my drive at home, but no, nothing, zilch.

My husband was around when I got in the house, and I hardly had time to take my coat off before he started excitedly telling me about a purchase he had made on an online auction site. I must admit, I find it really difficult to become enthused about the acquisition of some new gardening tools but in my husband's world these are big events, so I did try to put some effort into congratulating him.

The feeling that my 'real' life had taken over after crossing the threshold of my front door and, my 'other' life, the one filled with suspense and promise was now closed at least until 9am tomorrow morning was quite soul destroying. So, maybe that was the way to handle things, to divide my life into two compartments. The real one and the other one, each with their own dedicated time and space and as long as one didn't overlap with the other, then neither 'life' could affect the other. In that way no one else would know, no one else would find out, and no one else would get hurt. Right? The word adultery had started to jump into my head a few times, but I chose not to dwell too deeply on it. If I didn't analyse it, acknowledge it, or accept it then in my mind it wasn't happening. Right?

I have friends and colleagues who moan about their husbands and partners and the little that they help around the house with the mundane daily chores that usually still fall to the woman of the house. I had no such complaints or issues, and I felt that I should have shown a little more gratitude when my husband also insisted on showing me how well he cleaned the upstairs of our house. It was Tuesday, and this was 'upstairs' cleaning day for him. It wasn't that I didn't do any of the chores – I did do 99% of the cooking and shopping – it was that I still worked full-time, and my husband had been retired for a good few years and therefore had more time than I did. If the roles had been reversed and it was I who stayed at home all day and did most of the household chores and it was my husband who went out to work all week, would this be viewed in the same way? Compared to how much I used to do throughout my first marriage, particularly when my children were younger, I hardly ever get involved with meaningful housework these days. I remember thinking at that time that perfect husbands such as the one I had found just didn't exist.

Still, it wasn't and hadn't been plain sailing over the years. As good as he was at the domestic stuff, he was quite useless at other things which used to frustrate me greatly. For instance, he has never arranged or booked a holiday or even a weekend away. All of those things, which carried a degree of stress, were left to me to organise. Yes, he would take an interest in where we were going and when, but the phone calls, internet searching, taxis, transport, foreign currency and passports etc., etc., etc., were all my responsibility so I never really felt like I was being treated. He had never booked a restaurant or a day out, not even a suggestion of anything... I could go on and on and on.

On the positive side, and there aren't many, at least I had the full choice of when and where we went but with the positives also comes the stress, none of which my husband had to endure. I did, however, draw the line at packing for him although I may as well have done that, with the constant asking of my opinion and approval to whatever he was taking. It always ended up that he was told what day and date to be ready, get his coat and bag and the rest was sorted for him, by me. This was a luxury that I never got to experience.

It was now Wednesday and, frustratingly, I hadn't received any messages from Anthony. It was now nearly 11am. I began to think that my suggestion of a garden centre meet-up had not impressed him and he had gone off the idea and for some strange reason my feelings at that thought were caught between disappointment and slight relief. Both of these emotions were suddenly put aside when he eventually replied. 'Hi, that sounds perfect. I don't know the Terracotta Garden Centre, but no problem, I'll find it and see you there on Friday 2:30. Looking forward to it. BTW if I get there before you, is it tea or coffee or something else?'

'Coffee please' was all I could muster to reply. So, it was happening. It was on. I was relieved, anxious and excited in equal measure. One thing I did know was that if I wanted to finish work early on Friday, I needed to get my head down and get on top of things.

The remainder of Wednesday and all of Thursday went by without any further communications between us. I was completely engrossed by thoughts of what I should wear. What would be appropriate for such a meeting or, worse still, what would be inappropriate?

Friday morning arrived and as I shared a cup of tea with my husband before leaving for work, I wondered if I should mention to him that I was meeting a colleague for coffee later that day or would that revelation start a conversation that may not be in my best interests. What if he offered to meet me with my 'colleague'? He had never done this before and never before had the possibility of him suggesting it fill me with absolute dread. If I did mention it to him, should I tell him the full arrangements, time and place? I don't know if I was feeling guilt or fear, but I was feeling very uneasy.

Luckily, though, as the morning 'chat' continued, all three or four sentences of it, my husband interjected that he had planned to spend the day at his sister's house to help with some decorating – she was widowed and couldn't manage these tasks very well. More importantly, she lived over 70 miles away in the opposite direction to where we lived. I was hoping that he hadn't detected the relief that overcame me as he continued to say that he expected to be back late that evening and that he was taking our dog with him. His sister had offered to cook tea for them both.

I had managed to catch up with most of my outstanding jobs at work during Wednesday afternoon and Thursday, so Friday was quite light work-wise.

I had chosen an outfit to wear to work that would also be suitable for meeting with Anthony later on that afternoon. However, as I was finished everything that I needed to at work and it was well before lunchtime, and now with the morning information that my husband would be out for most of the day, I decided that I had the time to go back home and rethink my outfit... Perfect.

Were the stars aligning? Was this OK?

I changed from my chosen morning outfit into something less 'office-y', so black smart trousers and a pale blue cable knit cardigan, top three buttons undone, black shiny shoes and white blazer. Lots of bling and I was ready.

It was now approaching 1:30pm. It would take me approximately 40 minutes to get to our meeting place.

Plenty of time but I wanted to get into the car park first and wait in my car until I saw Anthony arrive, if he did. I wanted to observe how early he would arrive as this could be an indicator of his eagerness to get to our meeting, and see what he was wearing. I had spent ages planning my outfit so I would be a bit disappointed if turned up in an office suit or anything that didn't look like he had put some thought into it.

As I sat in my car, which I had parked slightly obscured from the main car park entrance, it struck me that I hadn't previously taken much notice of which car he drove. I knew it was a grey-coloured Audi Q5 but I didn't know the registration number. It wasn't that distinctive really so I shuffled around in my seat so I could see the entrance more clearly. My clock in my car said it was 2:15 and I hadn't seen him arrive yet; maybe he is already inside waiting. Keeping my gaze on the entrance, I decided I would go in at 2:40, which didn't seem too eager or too late.

At 2:23 he arrived. I hadn't seen him park his car so he must have used the busier side of the car park. My stomach flipped. He looked gorgeous even from this distance. A light blue shirt with sleeves folded back to just above the wrist to reveal his watch. Dark blue chino-type trousers. Definitely looked as if he had put some consideration into what to wear.

The cafe in the garden centre is almost to the back of the building, which is huge, so, as he had told me he had not been here before, I knew it would take him a few minutes to locate it and get a table. I pictured in my mind him looking around to see if I was already there. At exactly 2:30, according to my phone clock, a message from him arrived. 'Hi Sarah, I'm here. I've got a table on the right just as you walk in and I have ordered the coffees. See you soon'. There was no 'Ax' this time. As he had ordered the coffees before I was there, he was obviously confident that I would turn up, either that or he didn't mind having two coffees. Confident or arrogant or just a gentleman? There I go overthinking again.

'Just parked', I lied. But a thought crossed my mind – what if he had also been observing me from the car park and he would know what time I had actually parked? I had already started this fledgling relationship on a lie.

Just another minute adjusting and readjusting anything that I could, and I left my car and made my way to the cafe entrance. Just for a second, I couldn't remember whether he had said the table was on the left or the right then it came to me he said the right. This was it then, I was there.

I slowed my walk down and turned to the right and he was sitting facing the entrance. He was doing something on his phone so momentarily he didn't see me as I swished my hair and walked towards him. He looked up and broadly smiled, then he got up from his seat and with a welcoming arm he reached out. "Sarah," he said and kissed me on the cheek, "how lovely to see you."

I cannot remember sitting down on my seat as I was in such a fluster, but I obviously did sit down at some stage. Before too long the coffees arrived and thankfully the conversation started.

"It's nice to see you," he said, "this is a lovely place, have you been here before?"

"Nice to see you," I said. "Yes, I've been a couple of times but not recently." I then I waffled on, "It's nice to see people outside of their usual environment, people just look so different, don't they?" I had no idea where I expected this conversation to go.

"You look lovely," he said and then he followed that with, "I wasn't sure that you would come."

I thanked him for the compliment and asked, "Why on earth would you think that?"

"Oh, just a feeling," he responded.

I was nervous about holding eye contact although I did allow myself a flickering glance from time to time.

We managed to fill the next hour or so with inane topics of conversation around work mainly – at this time it was the only thing that we have in common – how we ended up working for the same company. The weather, cars and hobbies were all discussed with varying degrees of interest on both sides. The subjects of families, mainly husbands, wives, children or significant others was not touched upon at all.

For some reason I glanced at my watch, and he asked if I was OK for time or did I have to be somewhere else soon. I said no, but it was just gone 4pm and I was sure that the cafe closed at 4:30pm.

"Just time to fit in another coffee, if you could manage it?" he asked.

"Yes, why not!" was my answer.

He signalled the waitress and as she took our order, he enquired about the closing time and she told us that the cafe closed at 5pm.

"Looks like we are OK for time then," he said and smiled.

The reason that we were both there, the reason that we had both shown up today, was hanging in the air but neither of us seemed brave enough to mention it or bring it out into the open.

We got through our second coffee a little quicker than the first and at around 4:30 it had become noticeable that the cafe was thinning out considerably so he asked if I fancied a little 'mooch' around the garden centre for a while as that part didn't close until 6pm. I agreed that that would be a nice idea, so he settled the bill and we rose from our table and walked out of the cafe into the main area of the garden centre. I thanked him for paying for my coffees and then he replied that I could pay next time and then he winked. I wasn't sure whether the wink meant there was going to be a next time, or that I wouldn't be paying next time.

Neither of us were particularly interested in, or paying that much attention to, any of the things in the garden centre and I felt that the conversation was drying up a little save now for the odd comment on plants or pictures. As we walked around, our route led us naturally towards the exit and into a large glass foyer. I wasn't sure if this was going to be the 'handshake', thank you and goodbye moment, with a peck on the cheek for good measure. It was hard to tell but maybe I should be the decider on this, but I just couldn't think of a way to end the meeting.

As we stood in the foyer, Anthony turned to me and asked if I would like to continue our conversation in either of our cars as it was quite busy in the place where we were standing.

"Oh, OK," I said.

The car park had also emptied out quite a bit since I had parked earlier and, as we walked out of the foyer, it still hadn't been decided whose car this conversation was going to continue in. Should I insist on mine or should I insist on his? That question was soon answered as he took his car keys from his pocket and said, "I'm over here," pointing to grey-coloured Audi that I recognised now as the one in the work car park. I noticed that he had a personal number plate: 19 AMR.

It was a conversation starter, so I enquired about the number plate, and he told me that it had been a present from his parents on his 19th birthday (now both deceased).

"And the 'M'?" I asked.

"Martin," he said. "It's my dad's name."

With that, he unlocked the car and held the passenger side door open for me to get into. My entry onto the passenger seat fell short of being elegant as my handbag managed to wrap itself around a fixture on the bottom of the seat so I was glad that I had opted to wear trousers. We both saw the funny side and it went some way to breaking the ice.

"Nice car," was my feeble effort at starting the chat as he got into the driver's seat.

"Thanks," he said, "it's a lease one, it's easier and less hassle as I have to travel around a lot and it's also a bit of a tax dodge."

"Good thinking," I replied.

He shuffled around in his seat and asked me where I had parked and I pointed to a row of half a dozen or so cars at the very back of the car par. "That's me, the black Seat Ibiza," I said. "It's not fancy but it's new," I added.

I nearly said that my husband had chosen it for me as he usually had the final say in the choice of the family car after he had done his research and explored fuel consumption, insurance etc. But neither of us had, up until now at any rate, mentioned anything about our home and family lives or the people we share it with so I was glad that I held back from that.

So, there we both sat, side by side, in the quietness of his car, both nervously looking around and out of the windows. For my part, I was desperately searching for something to start a conversation with. For a second, we had both turned around to face each other, and as our eyes met it was becoming uncomfortably obvious that one of us either had to put an end to the afternoon or one of us was going to have to start a conversation... *The* conversation. I didn't really have any idea past this point how of I imagined things were going to go.

There was a brief moment of silence before he reached over to my lap and took a hold of my hand. I watched his hand as he wrapped his fingers around mine and brought it towards him. As we both looked up and towards each other, he said, "Sarah, I know why I am here today. I just need to know that you are here for the same reason." He continued, "Absolutely no pressure at all. I have had a lovely afternoon in your company; I just wanted to know that I hadn't read the signals wrongly."

I was hoping that he would keep talking as I was struggling to find a way to answer him. But there really was only going to be one way. "Yes, I think we are."

Goodness only knows what he made of that, but at that moment when his left arm came around the back of my seat and settled on the back of my neck and, with the gentlest encouragement, he moved my head towards his. I was powerless to resist him as he softly and gently put his lips onto mine. Although that first kiss was passionate, it was over quickly and as we pulled apart from each other I was embarrassed to look him in the eye. For some unknown reason I said, "Where did that come from then?" Without a word being spoken between us, we kissed again. At the touch of his lips on mine and his fingers in my hair I simply melted as if years of feeling bereft of attention and the famine of passion that I had settled for had just been repleted.

As we sat there, both of us seemingly slightly stunned, I turned to Anthony and said, "What happens next?"

He answered, "Well, I would certainly like to meet up with you again." He added, "I understand if you need time to think about things and where you would like to go next with this. It's in your hands, as am I."

My thoughts were jumbled, and my head was scrambled, and I could still feel his kiss on my lips, the feeling was intoxicating as I said that I would very much like to meet up again.

A smile came over his eyes as he said, "Thank God for that," and we both laughed at his answer. I looked at my watch once more, not that I had anywhere else to be. He must have sensed that a was preparing to leave when he said, "So, shall we make that arrangement now or do you need a few days to think about it and get back to me?"

I thought for a moment and then suggested that we meet here again in two weeks' time at the same time. I remembered that I had Thursday and Friday off from work during that week and even though my husband was aware that I had those days off, I could be absolutely confident that he wouldn't have any made any plans for those days. That was my department in our marriage.

"Perfect," he answered, and we both leaned in towards each other for our final kiss of the meeting.

He started his engine and drove the short distance around the car park to take me to my car, which was just as well as my legs were so shaky that they would have struggled to hold me up. He came around to my side of the car and, as I had made such a mess of first getting into his car, I was especially careful to wrap the handle of my handbag securely around my wrist before getting into my car. We both found it amusing as he kissed me on the cheek before he got into his car and left.

I felt totally drained, absolutely ecstatic, but completely panicked as I started the engine of my car. It was difficult to take in what had happened over the past couple of hours. I was driving back to my home, my husband and my family life as I had always known it, only this time I was driving as an adulterer. I was on the road to adultery and the journey to that destination had begun. I had checked my phone before starting off and there was only one message; it was from my husband. He was just letting me know that he had arrived at his sisters. His sister was cooking tea for them both so he wouldn't be back until late that evening.

The journey home was a bit of a blur. I wondered whether Anthony had thought of me and our time together this afternoon whilst he was driving home.

It was Friday and I didn't expect to hear from him again over the weekend. I suppose I could have contacted him but as we hadn't divulged anything to each other about our home lives and the people who we shared them with, but I didn't want to risk causing him any uncomfortable situations and I expect he felt the same way about contacting me.

The evening and the rest of the weekend were relatively OK considering where my head was at. It seemed that I was able to jump back into my 'normal' life and put my 'other' life aside quite easily. That's not to say that I hadn't re-ran that first kiss between Anthony and I over and over again and recall how he looked. I was trying and hoping to relive the melting feeling one more time. Although I had managed not to give any outward appearance of my distraction.

During the next couple of weeks, Anthony was in and out of the office on several occasions but we were both cautious about appearing to be too familiar with each other. I sent and received regular messages but only during office hours and I projected my thoughts to the upcoming second meeting that we have planned for this coming Friday. I had given a lot of thought as to bringing our outside lives into the conversation just to gain a little clarity as to the 'rules of engagement' as it were. I wondered if he was curious as to what I got up to outside of the office. When we last knew each other, some six or seven years ago, we both knew that the other was married but many things can change and happen over time – illness, divorce or death for example – and I was curious to find out whether any of these things had had an impact on his life. I was feeling that I could probe these areas in a way that I wouldn't have been comfortable with before.

The day of our second meeting arrived. I hadn't planned to be in work that day but something urgent had come up and I had to go in for a few hours during the morning. Anthony was also working. He passed me a lovely glance as he walked through the office... a knowing glance. I wouldn't have the time to get back home to change my outfit for this meeting as I had been able to do for our first, but I felt that what I had chosen to wear was suitable for the office and a coffee meet-up. I was planning on leaving work for 1:30pm to give myself plenty of time for my journey.

I had printed off some costings for the accounts department that were nearly overdue so, rather than rely on the internal post system, I decided I would deliver them myself to make sure the accounts department received them before the end of the working day. The walk to the department from my office was via a glass partitioned walkway that connected the two buildings, and it overlooked the staff car park. I was now familiar with Anthony's car, and I was unable to see it in the car park or, at least in the spot that I would have expected it to be. It must have been there this morning as we were both at work. Maybe he had left early to get ready just as I had done last time, I mused.

The traffic was a little busier than when I had last made this journey, and I was slightly later than I expected to be but still in time as I arrived at 2:25pm. It didn't occur to me to look for his car as I was a little flustered at arriving later than I wanted to. Last time he had messaged me to let me know that he had arrived and where he was sitting but, as yet, I had received no such message. I wasn't concerned about arriving before him this time, but it did seem odd that he hadn't let me know of his arrival, etc. as it was now 2:30pm.

I needn't have concerned myself as I could see him as I entered the cafe in the same seats as last time. He greeted me again with a lovely smile and a kiss on the cheek and I reciprocated by saying how much I had been looking forward to the meeting.

"Usual coffee?" he asked as the waitress approached our table.

"Yes please – you remembered?" I said.

"How could I forget, I remember everything," he added, and I felt a giggly blush come over me. The 'voice' had done it again and the butterflies returned on cue and in abundance.

The conversation went pretty much the same as the last one and I got the feeling that we were both in an unspoken hurry to end up in one of our cars. As I had predicted, he suggested that we not bother with a second coffee and the walk around the plants and pictures. Instead, this time, go and continue in the relative silence and privacy of his car. I did offer that we sat in my car this time but it seemed that he had almost taken the decision out of my hands and with that he pulled his car keys from his back pocket. We both remarked on whether I would make a repeat performance of clambering into his car this time as I had last time but I assured him, laughingly, that I was in control this time.

There was a light perfume in his car this time that I hadn't noticed on the last occasion that I sat in it with him. "Have you had your car cleaned?" I asked. "Is that why you left work early today?" After I had asked, it suddenly came to my mind that he might think I had been spying on him.

"No, I haven't been to the car wash," he answered. "I left work around one-ish for another very good reason."

I wasn't sure but I thought I detected a slight irked tone in his voice, but I didn't explore that any further. He then reached behind the passenger seat, where I was sitting, and produced the most gorgeous bouquet of flowers.

"I hope you will accept these and find a place in your home for them and think of me when you look at them."

I am not an outwardly emotional person and rarely cry. It's not that I don't feel emotion it is just that I don't find tears easy or helpful, but I must admit that I did feel the welling of emotion that brought half a lump to my throat as I took them from him. "They are lovely, such a lovely thought," I said as I reached to kiss him.

He responded with beautiful soft lips, the sort that catapults the receiver into a different time zone. "Lovely flowers for a lovely lady, I am glad you like them," he said.

I didn't have to worry about taking these flowers home as I always had to but my own flowers if I fancied any for the house – another thing that my husband would never have given thought to, not even on special occasions or even when I had spent a short time in hospital (nothing serious, just women's troubles).

I received flowers from my children, a couple of friends, and from work colleagues during this time but, no, nothing from my husband. He did most of the other stuff and housework which was a really big help and was very thoughtful of him so I was not ungrateful, it's just the little extras that he was no good at, the little extras that complete the picture.

Sitting in his car we continued to embrace, kiss, laugh, and chat, and I eventually decided to ask the questions that had been niggling away at me.

Still holding hands, my flowers now in the footwell between my knees, I asked, "So, what is life like for you after office hours?"

"I had been thinking the same about you," came his reply.

"You go first," I said, sounding very slightly insistent.

He continued to tell me that he was still married to the lady that I had met at our earlier meeting some years ago. It was a second marriage for both of them. His wife didn't have any children from her first marriage and they didn't have any children together. He told me that he had a daughter from his first marriage who had emigrated to Canada after marrying a service man who was posted there. He visited his daughter every other year and she came to the UK to visit him and her mother in the in-between year. He said that he and his current wife had grown apart over the past five years or so, and although they resided in the same house together, they lived essentially separate lives. Now, I don't want to appear unfeeling but is this the same shitty spiel that every married man looking for a bit of extra marital sex spits out? Was it a sales pitch?

He carried on by adding that it wasn't his domestic situation that had made him reach out to me, he said it was that he thought there had always been a 'sort of' connection that went beyond us being colleagues and that he now hoped would stretch beyond us being just friends.

There was a pause for a second or two as if that was my signal to give my side of things and an insight to the events that had led up to me sitting at his side in his car in a garden centre car park.

I started off as if I was in a job interview and was trying to sell myself. "I have been married twice and this time for 15 years, I began. I have two children from my first marriage who are both all grown up and have their own lives with their own partners. I see my daughter more often than I see my son, about half a dozen times a month or so." After that I really couldn't think of anything else to add. That was it, I was 56 years old, and my life could be described in a couple of sentences.

"Will the flowers be OK then, when you get them home?" said Anthony. I assured them that they would be fine as I regularly bought myself flowers and they were rarely noticed. "How could anyone not notice you?" he said.

And with that all out of the way, we shared the most enduring passionate kiss. I felt as if I was truly floating on air and with the touch of his hands on the side of my neck a load of other feelings and flutterings began to overload me, and him. The next step couldn't be far away, and I felt that we really had to discuss it soon.

As our mouths parted and we both took a minute to come back down to earth, Anthony asked me how I was feeling. "Confused and excited," I replied.

"We really need to talk about something, don't we?"

I replied, "Yes, we do."

As adults who had 'been around the block', we both recognised the sexual tension and attraction that was at a heightened level between us as we sat in his car. "Any suggestions?" he asked.

"Shall we meet up again soon and in the meantime we can both have a think about how we would like to carry this forward onto the next level if we want to?" I carried on telling him that I did really want to, in fact our next level hasn't been far from my mind for a while. I had played it over more than once in my head. I felt embarrassed as I admitted this to him. We decided to meet up again and one of us would contact the other with a suggestion for the day and time and with any ideas for moving forward.

Although I had spent decades being the arranger and the organiser for most other people in my life, I couldn't think of anything to suggest , but both of us came away from that meeting with absolutely no doubt that the 'next level' that we both had in mind would involve our relationship crossing the intimacy line.

As I drove home and back to my 'normal' life, any feelings of guilt that maybe I should have felt were blanketed by feelings of anticipation and excitement.

I hadn't found it difficult to move from one life to another as I returned to my normal life and its regimentation and routine. The bins would have been emptied, the lawns would have been mown and the yearly round of garden fence painting and maintenance would be well under way. Yes, the house and the garden would, as they always did, look pristine. As I pulled into the drive, my husband appeared form the back of the house and took my car keys from me in order to put my car in the garage. There was no chance of it being left on the drive – everything in its rightful, tidy place. There would be no greeting kiss or promising look in his eyes. I didn't really doubt that he was happy to see me home safe and sound, but any sign or possibility of him showing that was, as it had always been, out of the question – it would never enter his head.

I didn't make an issue over these things as it had always been the way with him – I had accepted that a long time ago – but it was only recently that I was starting to realise that I haven't been living my own life as me. I had been conforming to my husband's way of living. Everything neat and tidy, everything in its place, everything done on a certain day and at a certain time. Towels and bedding washed and changed every other Monday, big shop on Tuesday, fish and chips on Fridays. I had no objection to his routine; it was just that I found it boring to always live like it. But, on the whole, he was a good man and I let him think that I was OK with it.

I don't suppose everyone is the whole package, the real deal. Happiness can never be 100%, it has to be measured in whatever percentage of happiness you are happy with. I was probably at 65-70% and up to now it had been enough. My husband never showed any physical affection, he didn't give compliments, although he constantly sought them, he never instigated intimacy or touch of any sort. During our first couple of years together, it was always me who instigated anything sexual between us. I was the one who moved towards him in bed and put my arm around him. I would start the tender neck kissing, but it was rarely reciprocated. Eventually, with effort on my part, he would achieve an erection and sex would take place, without any foreplay of any kind being offered to me. Then, with a couple of inelegant grunts, it was completed, all over, finished. So there was very little to keep me interested, let alone coming back for more. It was, I felt, an awful lot of input from me with very, very little, if any, reward. Masturbation was a way of relieving some of the times of frustration, but it didn't satisfy the desire for skin-to-skin contact.

I had no intention of leaving my marriage or my home. I grappled with this – the notion that, as my husband and I had stopped having sex, touch or emotional contact, was it wrong for me to contemplate filling that void with someone else? I wasn't having or getting sexual stimulation or fulfilment with my husband so was it wrong for me to seek it from elsewhere? After all, I wasn't replacing my husband with someone else for this fulfilment, I was seeking it from someone else as he didn't want to do it. Was this really adultery? Or was it a right and proper justification in my desire to satisfy my needs and to make me feel like a desired woman and a whole person?

The weekend weather was lovely and sunny, and I spent a lot of time in the garden. We had invited our neighbours around for cheese and wine on Saturday evening; it was very enjoyable and helped the time pass more quickly. Sunday was OK; I took our dog for a lovely long walk on my own which gave me a welcome chance to be alone with my thoughts. I had the seed of a plan in my head about the next step for Anthony and I, but I had no idea yet of how much thought he had put into it. I decided to message him as soon as I got into the office tomorrow morning.

As I arrived at work I didn't know whether Anthony would be in the office that day as he hadn't said anything last Friday. I waited until around 10am and, as I hadn't heard from him, I decided then to send him a message. 'Hi, any thoughts re: Friday's conversation. Any possibility that we can meet this week to discuss further?'. And I signed it 'Sx'. It was around 10:30 when he answered my message asking me which day I was free during the coming week, and he added that he was free on Tuesday and Wednesday afternoons.

It was going to be difficult for me to have an early finish on either of those days, so I suggested to him that, if possible, we arrange an evening meet-up this time. I was so anxious to see him again, so I said that Tuesday evening after work was probably better for me and he replied that that suited him as well. As we were meeting in the evening this time, it meant that we couldn't go to our usual garden centre as they would be closed, so he suggested that we meet in the car park of a large cinema complex that wasn't far from the garden centre. He said we could get a takeaway coffee and sit in his car or on the benches if the weather was OK. I agreed as I didn't have any better ideas.

When I got back home on Monday evening, I didn't tell my husband that I would be later than usual the following evening. I just dropped into the conversation that I had a large workload to catch up with and I was lucky to have finished work on time this evening. I had sown the seed in his head, that's if he did manage to notice that I would be late home tomorrow.

*Oh, what a tangled web we weave, when first we practice to deceive!*

There were several empty benches in the cinema complex car park when we arrived almost together on Tuesday evening. It was a sunny if slightly windy evening but pleasant enough to sit outside for a while. Anthony was dressed quite casually in a pinkish and white two-tone rugby shirt with black chino trousers and I thought how attractive he looked as he made his way back to our table with the coffees. He laughed as he sat down as he said he had nearly bought me a hot chocolate but then realised that he didn't know whether I liked hot chocolate.

"I only know that you like coffee," he said, shrugging his shoulders.

It was a funny thought that we knew so little about each other. I thanked him for the coffee and remarked at how he had paid for all of my drinks at all of our meetings and told him that I did indeed like hot chocolate... Who doesn't? He smiled again and laughed that he had now doubled his knowledge about me and added that there was never a question that he wouldn't pay for everything while we were together.

There was a little more frivolous and flirty chat between us as we drank our drinks but as this meeting was going to be shorter than our earlier ones, and it had a defined purpose, the subject of any future plan was soon under discussion. He started off by asking me if I had had any thoughts and I told him that I had an idea... If he could get away for a couple of days then maybe we could book a hotel a little distance away and spend that time together. He nodded in agreement and said that he had had pretty much the same idea. He said he was hoping we could arrange something sooner rather than later, to which I nodded, and we went our separate ways. The cinema car park was a little too busy for us to sit in his car and end our meeting with a kiss as we usually did.

My husband never had any issues with me spending a few days away from home as I had done that quite regularly in the past with the occasional theatre trip or spa weekend spent with friends, or my daughter on occasion, and they would usually involve an overnight stay. I was aware, though, this time I couldn't claim to be away with anyone that my husband also knew just in case it ever came up in conversation at a later date.

So I decided that once the plans were in place and a date had been set between Anthony and I, then I would say that work had arranged a conference; it wouldn't be likely that my husband would be in the company of anyone from my office. So, half the plan was afoot.

My mind was now filled with things that I hadn't had to think about for a very long time, such as lingerie, underwear, and timely hair removal. I had always shaved my legs and underarms, but 'other' areas rarely got much attention. Teeth whitening also came into my thoughts as I wanted to set my stall for what was going to be our first time together and could possibly be our last.

I was on the internet quickly once the usual evening things were out of the way. I wasn't sure how soon I would need some new things, so I had to buy from a site that offered next day delivery. I decided to go with pyjamas – although I already had numerous sets at home, none of them were bought with this purpose in mind. Eventually I settled on a royal blue set in satin with a kimono-style wrap. The underwear choosing took much longer. Although they all looked very sexy, and they say they are what men prefer, I just couldn't bring myself to buy thongs and the bra with the cut-out nipples was a definite no go. I wanted to look appealing and sexy but also classy. It amused me that I hadn't put this much effort into choosing underwear for a long time and how styles have changed. The set, bra and knickers, had to be black and I chose a set with a lot more lace than I would normally wear, then *click* and they were ordered. Now the anticipation of waiting for the delivery.

If I am honest, I didn't really give much thought to a date, time or place that these purchases were intended for. I exhausted myself choosing them. As I showered that evening, I looked down towards my crotch which had developed into a mass of pubic hair. I only really shave my bikini line just prior to going on holiday. There was no way that I could present myself to Anthony like this, so I started to make an effort to tidy things up down there and it soon became clear that this was going to need more than one session. I had never considered a bikini line wax before, and I certainly didn't relish the thought now so I decided I would buy some hair removal cream tomorrow and try to achieve a tidier look with that.

My husband had managed to strain his back while he was gardening so he had gone to bed early to rest which left me with the evening to myself.

I wondered if Anthony had gone to this much effort regarding his night wear etc., then I thought, probably not as men just don't, do they? I thought it was more likely that he had spent time pondering on what I would be wearing and what he was hoping to do with me. Any sexual techniques that I ever did have had long since faded. I could probably still manage the basics. But surely if I am in bed with someone who is actually responsive then maybe all of that stuff will come flooding back naturally.

As my husband had put his painting trousers in the washing machine before he went up to bed, the timer had just buzzed indicating that the cycle had finished so I set about sorting them out and getting them onto a drying rack. I smiled to myself at the irony of my previous thoughts, of sexy underwear, and how quickly I was able to revert to my normal life.

Wednesday morning and another normal-ish day at work. Anthony's car was in the car park when I arrived that morning, although I hadn't seen him yet. Then a message came through. 'You look nice', it said, followed by a link to a website. His message continued, 'I've found this little place, not sure if it's your thing but have a look at the available dates and get back to me. If we decide to go, I was thinking Friday to Saturday'. Signed off with 'Axx' this time. It had been some time since he had signed off with his initial followed by a kiss, this time I had two kisses.

'OK', I replied. 'I will have a look soon and get back to you, so far it looks perfect'.

'Just like you', he sent back.

I smiled to myself, finished off the work that I was in the middle of and excitedly opened the link that he had sent. It was an Airbnb property called Rocky Cottage. It was on the Norfolk coast and it looked idyllic. From what I could see from the online pictures, it was just off a coastal path on the edge of a little village. I looked at the dates that were available; there were a few in May but it looked quite booked up after then. Prices for one night starting from £235.00. I messaged Anthony back and told him that the cottage was perfect and that I could do any of the available Friday nights in May and asked if there was a particular one that was more convenient for him.

It was a couple of hours before he got back to me asking if Friday 10th May would be OK for me. 'Sounds good' was my reply and as I sent it, I realised that we needed to sort out how we would pay for it – would we pay a deposit first?

I really needn't have troubled myself at all as just before I left work at the end of the day, I received a message from Anthony. 'All done – Friday 10th May. Hope that's OK with you. Let's chat later if we can. Axx'. I was completely taken aback as I had never – well, at least not in the last 20 years – had a man take the lead 'alpha' style and book anything himself. It was actually going to happen, what had been nothing more than a fantasy for all of these years was actually going to be a reality. I looked again at Rocky Cottage online and saw that he had booked the very first available date. This was to become our love nest for the night. I put it in my phone diary as RC10/05.

Three weeks and two days to go.

When I got home, I told my husband that there was talk going around at work of a possible conference. I added that the details had not yet been finalised, but it would probably be an overnight stay, possibly in Harrogate. I am not sure how I managed to roll this off my tongue without changing my expression, but I did, and, as usual going along with everything as he normally did, he said, "Lovely place, Harrogate, you will enjoy it." Not an iota of doubt or suspicion in his voice or on his face.

Don't get me wrong, I wasn't finding this lying a pleasurable experience, I wanted to be truthful. But how could I be? Why would I want to create hurt and upset to someone who had never caused me any of these things. Something in my head was telling me to come to my senses and halt this train of deceit before the inevitable wreck that was surely waiting down the line. I just kept justifying the whole thing to myself that, after all, nothing had happened between Anthony and myself yet and, may never do.

During the course of the next couple of weeks, Anthony and I shared a few messages a day. I always got a 'You look lovely' message when he was in and around the office and he had taken to signing off his messages with 'Ax10/05'. I took this to acknowledge the significance of this date between us. So that was it, 10/05 had now became our date – our code.

Panic mode sort of set in as the final days came around. I booked Friday 10th May as a day off from work as I didn't think there would be much concentration on my part and I wanted to book appointments to have my nails done and get a last minute blow dry for my hair.

Anthony and I hadn't discussed the arrival arrangements for the cottage although I had read that the online details stated arrival was from 3pm. I had already tried the postcode out on my phone and the journey was going to take me around one and a half hours. I assumed that we would be arriving separately. My thoughts then turned to supplies like food etc. As I had always been responsible for organising this sort of thing on my previous self-catering holidays with my husband, I had just reverted to type and started making a shopping list.

At this point, I decided to message Anthony and ask him if he had any info on these things, i.e. what was provided, if anything. Also, we hadn't discussed how we were going to pay for our stay. I assumed that as he had made the booking, he had at least paid a deposit, but either way I needed to organise a way of making my contribution. I signed off 'Sx10/05'.

He sent a couple of smiley emojis back in his reply and told me that everything had been sorted and all I had to do was get myself there, followed by a hug emoji and 'drive safely. See you at the cottage'. As I was reading that message another one quickly followed. 'Sorry to assume that you are driving yourself but if we can arrange it, I can pick you up and we can travel together'.

I thanked him for the offer but, on reflection, it was probably easier and better for us to travel separately. I added that I needed to know how he would like to split the cost.

He didn't reply for a while but when he did, the message read, 'Absolutely wouldn't dream of you paying for anything, my treat, your company is payment enough' followed by a range of heart emojis.

*Wow,* I thought to myself as I sat back in my chair, *this is a total alien situation to me.* I felt a little ungrateful as the feeling that I wasn't in control came over me, but

I was enjoying the excitement of the mystery that was set in place to unfold.

Thursday evening was spray-on tan evening which was a relative success considering it had been years since I had used any sort of leg makeup. Even though I wasn't sure exactly how much daylight my legs would actually see but the thread veins that accompany late middle-age had advanced too far to be left uncovered. I am certain that my husband wouldn't have noticed the odd tan smudge on the shower screen or towel and, if he did, he wouldn't comment on it. Despite my confidence, a cloak of guilt had surrounded me and, like a thief who was covering their tracks from a burglary attempt, I fastidiously wiped all of the surfaces in the bathroom. In a funny way it had started to become a pleasurable guilt.

In less than 24 hours, if all went to plan, I would be on the verge of sharing a bed and sharing a night with another man and possibly – hopefully – sharing experiences that I had desired for a long time but had placed into the 'bucket of never agains'. At 56 years old, my sex life, sexual desires and needs had been suppressed for nearly two decades in exchange for a quiet and comfortable life. What I had thought was dead was, in fact, only dormant only to be awakened by the chance meeting with someone who relit the dying embers and had the capability of causing an inferno.

I had set my alarm for the usual time on Friday morning and quite unexpectantly I had slept until it woke me. My husband had already gotten up, so I put my dressing gown on and went downstairs and made my way into the kitchen to find him sitting at the breakfast bar. A polite 'good morning' was exchanged between us. He knew that I wasn't going into the office early in order to prepare for the 'conference'. In an effort to reduce my feelings of guilt, I said I would walk the dog this morning.

"Will you have time?" he asked. "Do you have your travel plans and itinerary yet? Are you driving or going by train?"

All of these questions threw me a little as I knew that any answers that I gave would have been lies. Once again, I surprised myself with the ease at which I replied. "I have plenty of time, I have an appointment at 11am (I knew he wouldn't enquire as to what) then I will make my way into the office for the briefing." I finished by adding, "As far as I know, everything is sorted."

I consoled myself that two out of those three explanations were not too far from the truth. I made myself a coffee and we sat together at the breakfast bar and apart from a couple of comments about the daffodils being late this year, not another word was spoken. We didn't even look up from our coffee cups at one another. Life was as normal as it had ever been and therein lay the problem; it was perfectly and unstimulatingly boringly normal.

I finished my coffee, put some old clothes on, put the dog on his leash, and headed out for a walk in the local park. The weather was dry and bright but quite cool.

As my interactions, or rather lack of them, with my husband earlier in the morning had left me feeling a little flat, my thoughts soon turned to the plans for the day and evening ahead and I was beginning to feel impatient for it all to begin. I wondered how Anthony might be feeling, and I wondered whether his interactions with his wife this morning had left him feeling guilty and regretful about our plans. And, worse still, would he change his mind?

I had an appointment to have my nails done at 11am and then a blow dry at noon; I had left the hair appointment until the last minute as I wanted my hair to look as fresh as possible. I had chosen to travel smart but casual and just before I left the house I checked my overnight bag one more time. I knew my husband would never have looked in my bag but still I secreted my new lingerie and underwear in between my towels. I wasn't sure if towels were provided at the cottage, so I packed two bath towels, one for me and one for Anthony, old habits again rearing their head. I just couldn't get used to not having to think for someone else.

My husband was in our home office. It was really a spare box room that had some wardrobes in where we kept surplus clothes and other stuff, and it just so happened to have our computer, printer and a desk in there as well so we pretentiously referred to it as the office. I announced to him that I would be leaving soon. He wished me a good trip and asked that I let him know when I had arrived safely. Up to now, he hadn't asked which hotel I was staying at in 'Harrogate', so I was trying to avoid that conversation. He didn't come out of the office, not even to carry my bag down the stairs. I said I would let him know when I reached my destination, and I made my way out of the house. As I started my car and headed out of the driveway, I was overcome with a sense of freedom, total liberation. I was on my way.

As I was getting my nails done, the beautician was making small talk and asking the usual question of if I was I doing anything nice that weekend. I was so desperate to tell her what I was looking forward to, but I decided to keep the narrative of the workplace conference in Harrogate just in case she ever asked me about it again. The saying about good liars and good memories sprung into my head. I heard my phone vibrate in my bag whilst I was having my nails done but I thought it would look a bit ignorant to look at it while she was working and chatting away to me.

I hurried back to my car after she was finished to look at my phone. It was Anthony asking me how my day was going and letting me know that the keys to the cottage would be available from 3pm. He also said that he was hoping to arrive before I did but if, for any reason he was later than planned, there was a key safe next to the outdoor light and the number to unlock it was 6581. He signed off with 'See you soon' and a winking emoji, then I was off to the hairdressers.

I really didn't feel comfortable with not making any contribution to the weekend although Anthony had made it clear that he didn't want me to. I had made my mind up to take some nice wine and some special chocolates. The garden centre where we had first met had a department that did special selection wine (this wasn't a night for Pino Grigio), and handmade chocolates. It didn't seem a lot, but I didn't want to turn up empty-handed and I passed it on my way to the cottage. I chose two bottles of wine, one red and one white. I was unsure about the rose so I didn't bother with that. I also didn't know which Anthony preferred. The chocolate selection was equally as mesmerising – milk, dark, white, soft centre or hard – just how difficult could it be?

This problem had never befallen me before. When shopping for my husband, I knew exactly his preferences. This time was different as I was trying to choose something for a man with whom I was going to spend the night but whom I knew nothing about other than he didn't take sugar in his coffee. I didn't know his shoe size, his collar size or any basic details about him; he was in essence a stranger to me, yet he felt like someone that I had waited and longed for for a long time. Anyway, I ended up buying two boxes with a mixed selection, so I felt I had covered all bases.

Time had flown by, and it was now 2pm and I had wanted to be on my way to the cottage at least half an hour ago. In the car I used my sat nav on my phone as the one in my car would record the postcode in its history so I thought that by using my phone there was less likelihood of an uncomfortable conversation later. Anthony had messaged me again to tell me that the parking for the cottage was at the side of the house.

My journey was uneventful apart from some heavy traffic as I got closer to the coast but nothing disastrous. As the little chequered flag appeared on my phone sat nav the usual butterflies began to make their presence felt. These increased tenfold as I could see Anthony's car as I approached the cottage. He was out of the door to greet me before I could get out of the car. He looked amazing (jelly legs moment) wearing a cream-coloured light knit jumper and black Hugo Boss trousers. "You found it then?" he asked as he opened my car door and kissed me on the cheek when I had gotten out of my car.

"Yes, no problem," I replied, "it looks gorgeous, well done for finding it." He took my bag from my back seat and noticed the bag with the wine and chocolates in. "Not much, just a little contribution from me," I explained. He then replied that I was naughty and winked.

He ushered me in through the front door that led straight in to the sitting room which had a delightful cosy look and feel to it. I noticed a lovely log burner fire which was all set and ready to be lit. We then went through to the kitchen, and I noticed that there was a welcome pack on the table. "I took the liberty of ordering that in advance. Also, if that's OK with you, there is a small Italian restaurant in the village and I have booked us a table for 7pm, but if you prefer something else that can easily be changed."

"Italian is fine," I said as I took the wine from the shopping bag. Holding the white wine in my hand, I asked if he had found the fridge yet. He walked over to a pantry and there it was.

As he took the wine from me he said, "I hope you don't mind or consider it a liberty, but I have put some Champagne in the fridge as this is a sort of a celebration." I must have given him a funny look because he continued, "Well, neither of us are driving for the rest of the day, are we? It is ready now so shall I open it and you try to find some suitable glasses?"

I nodded in agreement and set about opening cupboards to find some glasses.

The cottage didn't have a garden but here was a small patio area at the back which was accessed through some French doors. There was a table and chairs. The patio area was separated from a patch of scrub land by a picket fence. There was a small gate and then a short path that then led to a footpath that weaved its way along the top of a cliff and that, in turn, looked over a small beach area. Although using this route to access the beach would entail quite a steep climb down and then the same steep climb back up. Anthony said there was a much easier route to reach the beach which went through the village and most people tended to use that so the path at the back of the house was rarely used.

This made it lovely and private, and gave a lovely view out to sea.

As we sat out on the patio drinking Champagne, I purposely positioned my hand in 'holding' distance and seemingly without any delay his hand was soon clasped around mine. Chatting away, we talked about the weather, the sea and the folks that we could see in the distance along the cliff path. I don't know if we were both avoiding the subject of us spending the night together, but we didn't discuss it. Anthony then very subtly mentioned that he hadn't shown me around the cottage entirely, so we took our glasses inside and he pointed to a staircase that was in the corner of the dining area.

This was a small, compact little cottage, and I suspected that it had probably been a fisherman's cottage at some time in the past. It was quirky in places but very charming and romantic. He beckoned that I go up the stairs first while he went to fetch my bag which was still in the sitting room. The cottage had two bedrooms with the main larger bedroom being at the back of house giving it a lovely view out to sea. As Anthony made his way up the stairs to join me, I was admiring the view from the window and suddenly the bed became the 'elephant in the room'. Neither of us mentioned it, instead talking about the decor and the view. The bed was a king size and took up a fair amount of space in the relatively small room. The bedding was beautiful and in keeping with the cottage theme.

Finally, Anthony broke the ice by asking me if I had a preference as to which side of the bed I would like to sleep on. We both laughed as I replied that I usually like to sleep next to the window. "So you are at the bottom then!" I realised that that the foot of the bed was near to the window. He then said that he thought he would sleep in the other room, I am not sure what expression came over my face, but he put his arm around my shoulder and said, "Only joking, unless of course that is what you want." We both sort of giggled in a way that, even without words, left no doubt as to where both of our intentions were cemented. Although nothing was being taken for granted.

We had about an hour to spare before we had to be ready to walk into the village to the Italian restaurant, so we decided to make the most of our lovely location and we walked for a while along the coastal path to the cliffs. Almost at once, Anthony took my hand and as we walked hand in hand and the atmosphere became much more relaxed. The conversation that we had was not very deep but it was flowing and I had a feeling of complete freedom and anonymity.

We returned to the cottage to prepare ourselves for the evening. The cottage had only one bathroom, but it did have two toilets. My pet hate is sharing a toilet, I think it is a middle-aged woman thing. There are certain things that become part of a middle-aged woman's life that should be known and seen only by her.

I was glad that I had packed a change of clothes. A button-through midi length denim skirt with a black ribbed top, loads of big jewellery, and black wedge sandals.

I quickly sent a message to my husband to let him know that I had arrived in 'Harrogate'. I also told him that everyone was meeting for dinner and if it turned out to be a late night then I wouldn't message him again tonight.

After I had finished freshening up in the bathroom, I went into the bedroom to get dressed. Anthony then went into the bathroom to also freshen up and he went into the spare bedroom to change his clothes for the evening. He appeared looking fresh with a light blue shirt and the same trousers as he had on earlier. He smelled intoxicating.

"You look smart," I complimented.

"Wow, you look fab," was his reply to me. "We are booked for 7pm but if we go a little earlier we can have a pre-dinner drink or two before we eat."

"Fine by me," I said as I gathered my jacket and bag.

Anthony picked up a jumper and we left. He locked the front door and we walked down the path and made our way towards the village, which was going to take us about 15 minutes. We held hands for most of the way. Again, the conversation was flowing but not deep, some subjects were clearly on the back burner for both of us for now.

We reached the restaurant which was bedecked in green, white and red, which is customary for most Italian restaurants. It was a small place with about ten tables of varying sizes downstairs; there were also seating upstairs. The waiter came to greet us as we walked through the door and Anthony took the lead by telling him that we had a booking for 7pm in the name of Randall.

This again was something that I wasn't used to as it had always been assumed when I was out with my husband that I would make the bookings and check us in when we arrived. My husband would always prefer to stand back and expect me to take over. Despite witnessing probably hundreds of men on various occasions doing all of the 'men' stuff, it would never have crossed his mind to do it. But that is how it had become, or rather how I had allowed it to become, probably because I just found it easier than trying to make him do or become someone that he just couldn't be. When it came to choosing furniture, my husband would much prefer to stand in the background and offer little or no opinion, therefore taking no responsibility, and it was me who interacted and negotiated with sales staff. To outsiders it looked as if I always got my own way and I got everything that I had chosen but this simply wasn't the case. He did, though, have the final say when it came to our choice of cars.

About four of the tables were already occupied and, as we were a table of two, they sat us in the bay window which looked out onto the street. As we perused the menu, Anthony offered to order the wine for us to which I readily agreed. We had already shared a couple of glasses of wine together earlier in the day, so I made a mental note to pace myself. It transpired that we were both 'pudding' people so we both decided to skip the starter and leave room for dessert. A selection of bread, oils and olives were complimentary, so they were placed on our table and we nibbled at them. The waiter poured a glass of wine for us, Anthony had chosen a red, and then we were left to consider our meal choices. We spent that time chatting about the meal, the restaurant, the cottage and the village.

I had to choose my answer carefully as Anthony looked up from his menu and asked, "Seen anything you fancy?"

Oh, how I could have answered that question. "Well," I said, trying to hide the half smile on my face, "as we are at the seaside and it says they use the local catch, I think I am going to go for sea food risotto. How about you?"

Anthony was still trying to make a decision and he eventually decided on a chicken pasta dish. He gave our order to the waiter and we were left to chat for a while. We clinked our glasses together and as I took hold of my glass my wedding and engagement rings 'tinged' on the glass. It seemed that any thoughts that I had about forgetting my normal life for a few hours were going to be met with the occasional reminder.

We both turned to look out of the window and then we both turned to look at each other. After what seemed like ages, but was probably only a few seconds, Anthony finally brought up the subject that had been hanging in the air all evening. Taking in a breath, he began, "Sarah, we are both adults and I think we both have the same reasons and intentions for being here tonight." I didn't know whether he was waiting for an answer but before I could say anything in reply, he continued, "Don't we?" Again, I didn't answer, I didn't know what to say. His eyes were prompting me for agreement, so I gave a shallow nod. "I expect we both have a lot of the same questions on our minds." Again, I nodded. "Not least the possible ripple effect of our actions which at some point will have to be addressed and dealt with one way or another."

I told him that I agreed with him but I felt myself becoming a little tongue tied as I tried to put a sentence together.

He then said, "I was wondering how you would feel about us not discussing any of the peripheral things while we are together for these couple of days. We have such a short time together to enjoy each other's company and neither of us knows what the next step will be if we both decide that there is going to be a next step. So, rather than dealing with the darker stuff shall we just try to put it all on the back burner until we meet and talk again after we have got back home?"

The sense of relief that washed over me that this subject had been brought up, dealt with and put away all in one sentence was overwhelming. I gratefully agreed.

For some reason, I thought, like me, he felt conflicted by what we were doing, or at least on the verge of doing. As a married man with commitments and a relatively nice and settled life against what he really wanted to do and the possible consequences that could manifest. In both our circumstances the situation was a double-edged sword. For one, not to have given in to this powerful drive to pursue the chance of fulfilment that was lacking in our lives and could be satisfied by each other for each other, would have kept the status quo intact and everyone, except ourselves, in our families happy.

I have heard that people ask why people who are contemplating extra marital 'attention' don't discuss their feelings and needs with their current partner. If I was looking at this from the outside, I would probably ask the same question. The thing is that my husband was not a coiled-up spring just waiting for the signal from me to unleash a typhoon of unadulterated passion and sexual activity into our life. No amount of talking, discussion or even pleading would have done anything... He just didn't get it... That I needed touch, passion and I needed to feel desired.

Compromise... What does that really mean?

I had compromised for nearly all of my marriage to my husband. I had accepted that he wasn't passionate, loving and sometimes he could be quite selfish. I hadn't asked or expected him to change in any of these regards, I just accepted him for who he was. That was my compromise, but where was his? He hadn't given one inch to meet me anywhere near even halfway in regards to my needs. It was as if, if my needs were ignored, dismissed and never talked about, then they didn't exist. But they did exist, they were very real to me, the only thing that was missing was someone to express an interest in them and, up until now, I hadn't found anyone that I fancied enough, and who fancied me, to fulfil them.

Love, lust, desire and want are deadly desires indeed, but was it really feasible to expect to have these human needs provided by just one person? And was it really a sin to take up the offer of fulfilment of one or more of these needs if they were being offered by from someone else? Especially if the acceptance of that offer is not intended to break up the life and family that you have created with someone else. A dilemma indeed. As I looked across the table into Anthony's lovely eyes and his voice like melted chocolate, I knew there was no going back for me now.

With that subject now out of the way, the air between us felt lighter and as we clinked our glasses again, the meals arrived.

We ate our meals, which were lovely, and we chatted and joked about people and work situations past and present, and things started to feel quite normal. We were a normal couple at last, if only for a few hours.

We finished our meal; the wine was finished as well. The waiter asked if we would like to see the dessert menu. We declined. I don't know whether it was because the meals had been large or whether it was our eagerness to get out of the restaurant and get into our own little space in the cottage that was the deciding factor, but we decided not to have desert. I reminded Anthony that I had bought some chocolates with me. Anthony asked for the bill and presented his credit card to settle up.

We held hands as we walked back to the cottage and we chatted about the meals and the restaurant. I told him that he had made a good choice. We seemed to get back to the cottage a lot quicker than when we had made the reverse journey.

There was a giggly excitement between us and, as Anthony unlocked the front door, we both stepped inside the house. As the front door closed behind us,

Anthony took a hold of me, my back against the wall, and we shared the most passionate kiss which was full of promise. I felt dizzy and completely lost in his presence. His mouth was now kissing my neck, and he was kissing his way down my cleavage. All of those years, all of those messages, all of those moments in the car park and all of the sexual tension that had been created was now here and ready to be released. The gates of what we had both been denied had now opened and the force of the flood was unstoppable. This level of passion had never been given to me so freely before and it was so easy for me to respond. We both recognised that, before too long, we would have reached the point of no return. I had meticulously planned, in my head, the way this night would play out and I also didn't want to lose the surprise of my new lingerie. We pulled ourselves apart and caught our breath.

The night was showing great promise but I didn't want to rush things and everything to be over in a flash, and there was certainty the possibility of that.

"Shall we finish the Champagne?" I asked. "And maybe try the chocs."

I have no idea why I even suggested that as food and drink were the last things on our minds. Anthony agreed to my suggestion and remarked that it was now probably too cool to sit outside as we had done earlier. He lit the log burner while I fetched the champers and chocs. There was a television in the sitting room but we didn't turn it on. We sat together on the sofa. Sometimes Anthony had his arm around my shoulder and sometimes we were holding hands. As the fire got going it lit the room with a lovely glow.

As we neared the end of our drinks there was now really no other reason to stay downstairs. I took the initiative and pointed to our empty glasses and said, "Shall we?" The meaning behind that question needed no further explanation.

Anthony then turned, took me by the shoulders and looked straight at me with a serious look on his face as he said, "If at any point you think this is not a good idea, then that's fine, you just let me know."

I thought how crazy he must be if he thought I was going to back out of any of this. I didn't say that, of course, I said, "Thank you, you too."

I asked if he minded if I used the bathroom first. "Absolutely not, ladies first," he said.

My plan was to have an all over freshen up wash, and clean my teeth, and while Anthony was in the bathroom I would be putting on my new lingerie and be in the bed before he appeared. My plan worked like a dream.

Anthony came from the bathroom wearing a T-shirt and shorts – not really sexy but, then again, I wouldn't have wanted him to walk in naked. He pulled the curtains across the window which darkened the room a little bit but as it was still light outside, we weren't in complete darkness. As he pulled his side of the duvet back and climbed into bed, he reached over and turned the small bedside light on. It didn't give much illumination, about as much as a couple of candles.

As he got himself settled, he noticed my bra. "You look gorgeous," he said.

"Thank you," I replied.

We were sort of half sitting up and half lying down. He leaned over towards me and I turned to him and, without a word, that all-encompassing kiss started again. As we wriggled to lie down, our bodies touched. The kiss continued where it had left off and, not that I would have wanted to, I was powerless to resist. I felt as though I was having an out of body experience, and the woman who was receiving all of this passion wasn't really me. His hands were softly feeling my body through my lingerie, tempting and teasing. I helped him take off his T-shirt, I stroked his chest then lowered my hand into his shorts. He gasped with a sigh of pleasure. He was already ready, erect, warm and inviting. It seemed that his hands were multiplying as my whole body felt caressed at the same time. The pleasure was indescribable.

Words seemed unnecessary as his tongue had now taken over from where lips had been and, as he worked his way down below my naval (I had never experienced this pleasure zone before), he carried on slipping his hand into my knickers, caressing my bottom and, with what seemed like one swift move, he removed my pants. I could hardly contain myself as his tongue got closer and closer with each delicate kiss and replaced his fingers. I had parted my legs, but I didn't realise that I had until I felt his head between them.

After a few minutes, I felt I wouldn't be able to control myself for much longer so I pulled his face up towards me and kissed his mouth with a passion that I didn't know that I possessed. The taste was absorbing and irresistible. I was now beginning to understand a lot of things that I had heard and read about before but found hard to believe.

We sort of jostled for position as we reversed the roles and he relaxed back into the pillows while I took charge and used some of the long-forgotten techniques I recalled to give him somewhere near the pleasure that I had just experienced and was still in the throes of.

It did occur to me at some point that this rush of pleasure was, in some way, due to the fact that maybe we both had it in our minds that our chances of meeting up like this were going to be few and far between – if it ever did happen again. We were doing everything that we had imagined doing on this one, and maybe only, occasion.

I had waited and fantasied for years for this chance. This was my chance, and I was going to take it.

Then, he made it happen, the two of us were now one. I was just so heady with the pleasures that he had bestowed on me that I was happy to just let Anthony carry on at his pace. As I became aware that the crucial moment was close, I opened my eyes and looked into his face as he was looking down on me. He was enjoying me, his eyes were full of me and at that moment I, and only I, became his world.

Exhausted in the post coital moments, we lay in each others arms until I felt my eyes drifting shut.

Sleep soon followed and we both slept well till dawn.

We were a little more adventurous with positioning during the morning intimacy. I couldn't imagine the passion, pleasure and sheer joy of last night being repeated, but this time as we were both aware of each other's bodies and, with the initial embarrassment out of the way, the pleasures were different, exploring, and had the same result for both of us.

Anthony made us coffee and brought them to the bedroom, and we sat in bed talking for a while and shared some very intimate kisses, then we decided to get up.

The welcome pack that Anthony had arranged for us contained some croissants and jams so we decided to have these for breakfast and sit out on the patio at the back of the house. It was a bright but cool morning so we each got ourselves a blanket from the spare room and sat all wrapped up together to make the most of our time at the cottage as the check-out time was coming around all too quickly.

We each had a quick shower, which we would have shared had the shower cubicle been slightly bigger, and started to get our bags together. The empty Champagne bottle waiting to be put in the bin seemed symbolic. The receipt for the restaurant meal and some empty chocolate wrappers. I seemed to have made an emotional connection with them all and I wanted to keep them and preserve the memories of our time together. But I knew that they, and the Champagne bottle, needed to be discarded and out of view with the memories staying fresh and forever alive in my mind where they couldn't be seen and therefore wouldn't have to be explained.

As 10:30 was fast approaching, we were ready to leave, our bags were in the sitting room. We held each other in a close embrace and seemingly endless kiss. "I wish we had longer here together and that we could stay," he said.

"Me too," I replied.

Even if the cottage had been available for us to say for another night, we both knew that we were treading a fine path and it wouldn't be wise to risk the chance of the whole relationship, or what there was of it so far, being cut short owing to an ill thought out rush of blood to the head. But I wanted it so badly.

Neither of us had brought into any conversation the possibility of repeating our stay at the cottage again. Bags in hand, Anthony said, "What a difference 24 hours makes." As he put his hand on the front door handle to open it, he pulled a sad face.

I tried to lighten the mood by saying, "If we don't go, then we can't come back." And then I chanced, "And I would love to come back."

"I didn't dare suggest it." he said, "in case you thought it presumptuous of me, but yes please, I would love to do this again and soon."

I felt so relieved that this may not be our last time here together so I said we would talk after the weekend. With one final loving embrace we walked out of the front door, down the path and left Rocky Cottage as we made our separate ways home.

For the start of the journey home, Anthony was on the same road as I was, but as he drove faster than I did he was soon out of sight. I thought I had better stop at the next available stop and check in with my husband to let him know that I was on my way home. Unsurprisingly, there had been no messages from him over the time that I had been away. When he answered the phone, he asked if I had been stuck in the traffic. I told him that the roads had been clear and the traffic wasn't heavy. He replied, "You were lucky," and then he continued to say that there had been traffic reports all morning regarding an accident that had closed the road that he was expecting that I would be travelling on.

A cold shiver then a hot sweat came over me as, once again, it rolled off my tongue that I probably missed it as I had taken a detour to give someone a lift home. The harsh face of deceit was again rearing its ugly head. I was just about to ask if we needed anything from the supermarket as I intended on calling in on my way back, but he had already put the phone down. He often did that once he had finished his part of the conversation, so frustratingly selfish. With the 'traffic' information still in my head, and the reasons that I had given for not getting caught up in it, I thought I had better look at the route map on my phone in order to have my story straight if he asked me anything further about it.

I passed a large out-of-town shopping complex on my way back which I had noted when I was travelling the other way yesterday. I needed some fuel and I could have done with a coffee so I decided to park up and have a look around the shops.

As I turned off my engine, I sat back in my seat and contemplated the events that had unfolded over the past 24 hours. It all seemed quite unbelievable, the future was uncertain and, quite probably, I would have to settle for this one and only occasion. The enormity of what had happened, to both of us, couldn't be underestimated. Not just physically, the boundaries that had been breached given that we were both married, but also the emotional enormity. Could we, could I, now just walk away and be satisfied with just the one time when my mind, body and soul were crying out inside for the touch of his presence once again. Maybe that was it and maybe I just had to accept it and remember the positives, but would I ever really be content with just that, and would he? It was the thing that I wanted, needed and desired the most in the world at this time. At my age, I knew that I did have the emotional resilience to accept that Anthony and I had had our time, if that was how it was going to be. We had planned it, orchestrated it and executed it without any repercussions as yet. So, would we be being foolish to even try for a second (or more) time.

Once seemed to be the most sensible option, but would it have been enough?

Yes, it was enough that in those endless, yet, at the time, fleeting hours, it was me. My skin that felt his touch, nervous, yet somehow knowing. My whole body that felt his breath, warm and tingling. It was my mouth that tasted him and his mouth, responsive and tender, and as he slowly yet determinedly created one from the two of us. It was me that was in your eyes. In those final moments it was me, and yes, it was enough.

Meeting me when I arrived home was the usual flat greeting that I had become accustomed to and that was then followed by my husband beckoning me into the kitchen. He was giving me a second-by-second account of his activities while I had been away. Pressure washing the driveway, painting the shed and mending the wheelless wheelbarrow to mention but a few. Not a single enquiry as to how my 'conference' had gone. I was more relieved than bothered that he hadn't asked me as I would have had to lie. This was his usual way of greeting me whenever I returned home from anywhere, as if anything that I had done or anything that I had to say was totally irrelevant. Such a contrast to the past 24 hours.

During my stop at the shops, I bought some ingredients for a chicken curry so that is how I spent the rest of my afternoon and evening. We ate our meal in the usual silence and, after clearing away, I went upstairs to unpack my bag and have a shower. I was unpacking my bag when I came across last night's lingerie and the memories that came flooding back filled me with a warm glow. I looked at my naked body in the bathroom mirror before I showered. It looked like my body but, of course, it felt different. I now felt that I had the body of a woman. I had experienced the pleasures and the pleasure zones that I thought were dead to me.

I went to bed saying that I was feeling tired from the late-night conference and the driving. My husband followed upstairs some 15 minutes later. Of course, he was more exhausted than I was, this was another selfish trait that he would display. He never asked if I was tired.

When we are in bed he turns on his right side with his back to me or he lies on his back with his hands across his stomach, and he manages to hold that pose all night. Our bed is a super king size so, with him on one edge and me on the other, there is a gulf of space between us that never gets bridged.

Only last night I was lying enveloped in the arms of a man that I barely knew, but had given me more pleasure, more stimulation, and more fulfilment in one evening that my husband had in nearly 20 years.

THIS WASN'T MARRIAGE, THIS WAS A LEGAL COMPANIONSHIP!

We had both made vows but neither of us, in our own way, had upheld them. This may sound like a justification, but it was an absolute fact.

On Monday morning, I took the initiative and I messaged Anthony as soon as I got to work. It had seemed ages since I had seen him. My excuse was to thank him for the lovely time that we spent together. He messages me back, almost immediately, to say how much he had enjoyed it also and he added that I had been in his thoughts over the weekend. He said he was in the office today and he had to attend a couple of meetings during the morning but he would contact me some time in the afternoon.

There was a sort of calmness now between us that had replaced the 'jumpiness' that used to be there before Rocky Cottage. True to his word, he contacted me mid-afternoon and he asked if we could arrange one of our coffee meet-ups soon. He ended his message with 'we have a lot to talk about' and signed off with his usual 'Ax10/05', so the code was still in place. We decided, over the following few days and messages, to meet up on the following Friday at our usual garden centre.

We arrived, almost together, and met each other in the car park and made our way into the cafe. Anthony signalled to the waiter to order our usual drinks. It was our first proper meeting since our time away. As we looked at each other and engaged in light conversation, I wondered if Anthony, when he looked at me, recalled our intimate time together. These recollections were certainly flooding around my head.

"How are you?" I asked.

"Just about recovered," he replied, and we both gave a knowing smile to each other. I reminded Anthony that he had said that we had a lot to talk about. "Yes," he said with a slight hesitation in his voice. "I do think we need to have a conversation about how we both want to consider our next move, always assuming that you want a next move," he said.

I nodded in agreement and said, "You're right, and I would very much like a next move please."

Anthony said he thought that the cafe was a bit too public a forum for such a chat so he suggested that we finish our coffees and continue the discussion in the privacy of his car. Again, I nodded in agreement to that suggestion, and we continued talking about work stuff and a few other insignificant things for half an hour or so until we had finished our drinks. Then we walked out of the cafe and made our way across the car park to Anthony's car.

As I settled into my seat, he leaned over and gave me another one of those lovely kisses, the 'fire' was stirring again, and he said he had waited all weekend to do that. I admitted that he had been on my mind a lot since last weekend and that it was lovely to be with him again.

"So, where do we go from here?" he asked.

I started to reply that I was so happy to have him in my life and the last thing that I wanted was to wake up one morning and find that we hadn't been able to sort something out where we would be able to continue our normal lives and also find time for each other. I continued that it all depended on whether he was feeling the same way.

Holding my hand, he said, "You have taken the words out of my mouth as I was thinking along those lines also."

We agreed that, while we both we enjoyed our coffee meet-ups, we were both a little 'long in the tooth' to resort to fumbling around in car parks and neither of us was going to settle for anything less than what we had experienced at Rocky Cottage. For me, it wasn't just the sexual experience that Anthony and I gave to one another, it was the intellectual conversation, which there was a complete lack of with my husband. Again, I nodded and asked if he had considered a solution.

He said, "Can I run this scenario past you?"

"I am all ears," I replied.

He carried on that, as our time at the cottage had been so special for both of us, that we made that our 'special place' and continue to meet for a night, or two if we could manage it, every year on the Friday that would be the closest to the 10th of May every year. He also added that we could always continue with our coffee meet-ups whenever we could arrange it but, it wasn't really feasible for either of us to make random sporadic plans to meet up as there was more chance of other people becoming aware of our connection and the repercussions that would cause.

Anthony and I both had the unspoken intent that we didn't want to break up our lives as they were outside of each other. I didn't want to leave or divorce my husband, and Anthony never gave any indication that he wanted to end his marriage. We were not intending to 'replace' our current partners with each other. We were not replacing anything except the absence of the basic human need to achieve sexual and intellectual fulfilment. We found both of those things in being with each other.

I digested what he had said and after a little thought, I began to think what a good idea it was. We would still be in each other's lives plus we would always have a definite arrangement to look forward to and be together, albeit only once a year. I could see how it would work.

He was looking at me quizzingly, so I said I thought that was an idea that would solve the problem of how we could continue to be in each other's lives. I insisted, however, that we share to cost of renting the cottage and as he had paid for the last weekend, that I book and pay for our next time. His expression gave the impression that he didn't really agree with this, but eventually, hesitantly, he agreed. So, '10/05' became our time.

After another beautiful kiss, he said he was so glad that we had got that sorted and he reached into the glove compartment and produced a small bag tied with a green velvet bow. "I wanted to mark that May is going to be our special time and I hope you will accept this and think of us and our times together whenever you wear it."

My breath was taken away as I took the bag and started to untie the bow. I could hardly speak but I managed to say that he was lovely and I was feeling very humbled. Inside the bag was a green satin-covered box and I gasped as I lifted the lid to reveal the most beautiful white gold bracelet with a small emerald stone. Anthony explained that the emerald stone was actually the birth stone for May, and he added that, as our relationship had been 'born' in May, it was to symbolise our union.

Speechless for a while, I finally said, "I really don't know how to respond to your kindness. It is beautiful in every way, including thought. Thank you so much." I leaned over and kissed him, and he then helped me to place it around my wrist. I just couldn't stop looking at it and felt very content that I would now, even in times of absence, have a reminder of him and our times together. We closed off this meeting with some lovely hugs and kisses and went our separate ways home.

He was right in that, if we continued down the path of secret, stolen moments in random car parks and satisfied each other with fumbling gratification then we would be categorising our time together as an illicit assignation and it certainly wasn't that, at least not to us. We had both appreciated the consideration that we needed to show to both of our significant others, who shared our lives everyday, but also give consideration to our need to be together from time to time to satisfy something that was lacking elsewhere, and with that satisfaction we both become better people.

Over the next few weeks, we shared many messages, and the occasional coffee meet-up. I had googled Rocky Cottage and as it was listed as an Airbnb property, I was able to pay a deposit and reserve it for the following year on Friday 9th May. I wanted to get that sorted ASAP as I had made it clear that I wanted to pay for our next time at the cottage. Like an excited child, I waited for the confirmation of the booking to come through and then I sent a screen shot of it to Anthony with a big heart emoji and signed off with our new code 'SX10/05'. The 'code' had now become the regular way in which we signed off our messages and it had become so important to me that I changed all of my significant numbers to it. For example, my phone unlock number now became 1005 when previously it had been, for years, my house number, my bank PIN was now our code, my work locker code was changed and my PIN for my computer had also became our code, So, whenever I used a PIN, I had a lovely reminder of Anthony and I and, of course, there was my lovely bracelet which I rarely took off, and, at times when I didn't wear it, it was in my bag, so he felt always somewhere close.

Our arrangement worked well, probably better than we could have expected, and it became part of our lives for the next nine years. Rocky Cottage became our haven once a year where we spent some beautiful, daring times together. We were lucky that the cottage was always available for the dates that we wanted it. Every time I walked into the cottage, even though it would have been the best part of a year since my previous visit, I got the feeling that it was waiting for us.

We continued to share the booking costs and I paid for the even numbered years and Anthony paid for the odd numbered years.

In the later years, our time there did not always include sex; it was not and never had been a prerequisite. It was just in those first few years we couldn't keep our hands off each other.

We found fulfilment and stimulation in one another's company and each other's intellect became equally as satisfying. There were still loads of hugs and kisses and beautiful quiet times.

Time and the years rolled by.

I was now 66 years old, and Anthony was in his 70th year. We were now at year nine in Rocky Cottage. There had been a few changes to the cottage over the years and to the village. We still went for walks along the coastal path. Our Italian restaurant had closed down a couple of years ago, but we still sometimes went out to eat and sometimes we would cook at the cottage.

The two of us had also changed over the years. Thankfully no huge issues regarding our health. We had by now both retired from work, so we didn't have that as a common interest for conversation, but we always found it easy to talk about other stuff. I looked at him over the breakfast table, the smile and the eyes were still the same, the commanding voice had softened a little but was still capable of sending my tummy into butterfly heaven. His face was older but so was mine and there was no denying that we were both approaching our twilight years.

We had been extremely lucky that ninth year as the weather was beautiful, warm and sunny and we spent a lot of that weekend outdoors. Sex didn't happen but that had lost its importance over the passing years, and we spent the nights sleeping contently wrapped in each other's arms. Whichever way that I turned during the night I could feel the reassurance of his arms around me. We parted in the usual way with a long, loving embrace and went off, until next year, to our homes and lives.

As I arrived back home, my husband was in the garden. He waved to me as he saw my arrival through a side garden gate, but as was normal he didn't come to greet me with a kiss or anything.

I made myself a cup of tea and as I sat out on the garden bench enjoying the sunshine and relaxing after my drive back from the cottage, I looked at my husband, and noticed how he had changed. Maybe I hadn't noticed the changes that much as we saw each other every day but his face was older, although his eyes and smile were the same. I reminisced at how it was his smile that I first found attractive about him. He was nearly 75 years old now and walked with a very slight stoop and was also a little slower.

We were also approaching our twilight years together.

He didn't sit with me while I drank my tea, instead he was up and down always finding something to do rather than engage in conversation with me. He hadn't changed at all in that way over the years.

I had taken some seeds from a couple of the shrubs that grew in the garden of the cottage, and I set about finding a suitable place to plant them in my garden. I looked around the garden and it was an absolute picture, a masterpiece, quite simply stunning. I hadn't ever appreciated the toil and effort that it must have taken my husband to achieve this. My husband had never been able to show me any physical affection, he had never said that he loved me and rarely complimented me on anything. As I looked around the garden, I began to realise that this was his love for me. Every flower, every bulb, every shrub planted with love to provide me with a beautiful garden and home which were, in fact, filled with love, but not the spoken kind, and it was only now that I was beginning to see it. It had actually been here all along.

Throughout the next few months, messages between Anthony and I became fewer and the time between them became longer. There was no real reason for this. I didn't ask him why and he didn't ask me, it just seemed a natural progression. I still wore my bracelet and we still signed off the messages in the same way with our code '10/05'. Everything was still the same, but different. That date seemed such a long time ago now.

The next time we were due to go to the cottage it was my turn to book and pay but, whereas I always booked the cottage again almost as soon as we had left it, I just kept putting it off until I decided that I wasn't going to book it again for what would have been our tenth year.

Anthony never questioned as to why he didn't receive the usual screen shot of the confirmation of booking that I always sent to him, not even as the time drew nearer and nearer.

The summer came and went as did Christmas. There were no heart emojis sent or received on Valentine's Day between Anthony and I as there always had been. By the time May came around, Anthony and I had not communicated for some months. If we had still been going to the cottage then, in this tenth year, we would have been going the following Friday on the 7th of May.

I had probably known for the best part of a year that we wouldn't be going to the cottage again and I wondered when it would have been that Anthony realised it as well. I couldn't put a reason on why I decided not to book the cottage again, I just didn't want to.

Something had changed as I had arrived home from the last time. I hadn't suddenly fallen in love with my husband, and I hadn't had an all-consuming attack of guilt, I actually didn't feel guilty at all.

Anthony and I never spoke of love, nor did we talk about forever.

I needed sex, I needed physical affection. But that's what these things are, they are needs, very necessary needs.

Love does not have to be, or need to be, physical, it can be shown, given and received in many other ways. I just hadn't looked properly. This is not to say that Anthony and I would not have happened, he treated me well and was a fantastic person, but the person who loved me, the person who supported me every day was the man I was married to, and his hard work and dedication to our home and garden kept us secure.

I had not had any sexual relations with my husband during the time I was with Anthony, and not in the many years preceding then, so I didn't see it as a betrayal to my husband.

I began to see my husband in a different way and with the arrangement that I had had with Anthony for nearly ten years always at risk of discovery, I decided there was nothing to be gained from carrying on.

Yes, I had lied.

Yes, I had been deceitful.

Yes, I had fabricated things on a mega scale.

But what if I had told the truth?

Probably, by now, I would be a divorced and lonely woman.

Anthony and I had never discussed leaving our homes and partners because we never intended to.

Children would be unhappy and divided.

Grandchildren would be unsettled.

What was the point?

It was only me staring out at my pristine lawns and garden. Hurt and upset.

It was only me who was feeling bereft at the loss of someone who had, for a long time, given me so much and made me a whole person for the time that we were together.

He gave me the sanity to be able to continue with the existence that I had excepted.

I wholly deserved this pain.

We knew our time was not infinite.

Death, disease or common sense, one of these would be the decider in how this all ended. I decided it would be common sense.

Our time was over.

After ten years our chapter had closed.

I never knew what the future, or fate, had planned for Anthony.

We never saw each other again.

## THE END